Looking for the Seams

by Brandon Currence

ISBN 978-1-64663-315-9

Published by

3705 Shore Drive
Virginia Beach, VA 23455
800-435-4811
www.koehlerbooks.com

looking for the seams

BRANDON CURRENCE

VIRGINIA BEACH
CAPE CHARLES

*To my wife, Nancy, who patiently watched
as I sometimes wrote late into the night.*

table of contents

CHAPTER 1

stanford

"Trip! Focus, kid!"

"I'm trying, Dad," Trip said with an edgy tone he had never used with his father.

"Well, if you don't get your mental game in gear, you'll have lost this match before it begins," Joseph said as they walked out of the Stanford University locker room toward the tennis courts. "Keep focused on your serve, son. Frank has done a remarkable job with it this season, so capitalize on that like we talked about. That's all you need to do."

Trip couldn't shake his anxiety. "I just don't think I can beat Heath. I've never beaten him, and I'm afraid I'm going to let the team down."

Joseph softened his voice. "Trip, don't worry about beating him. Heath's never seen the new serve Frank has helped you with, and no player in college tennis has a serve like yours. Didn't the radar gun top one hundred and thirty this morning? Heath can't touch that. Just win your service games and be patient until Heath falters on his service game, then pour on the heat. Be patient for that opportunity. Can you do that?"

Trip took a deep breath. He knew his father was right. "I'll do it, Dad," he said, trying to convince himself.

Walking onto center court at Stanford's tennis arena for the NCAA championship match, Trip Furman glanced up into the stands to see if his new girlfriend had shown up as promised. Mishael, a music major at the university, had not only shown up, she had filled two rows in the bleachers with friends rooting for Trip, waving red flags with a large white *T* emblazoned on them, and wearing matching red T-shirts. Trip's heart soared. He waved at her, then bowed to the fans. They immediately stood, cheering as loud as they could and catching the attention of the entire arena with their frenzied flag waving.

Trip watched as his father joined his tennis coach, Frank Hornbrook, in his box seat. Knowing this was his last appearance of the season, Trip went over and shook Frank's hand, thanking him for a great season. With Frank's coaching, Trip had led the Stanford team to the finals. Stanford was now tied with Florida State, led by Heath Whitman, and if Trip could win here, Stanford would be national champions. He went to his bench and waited for the pregame announcements and warm-ups.

Trip had come to Stanford for his masters after playing two seasons for the University of Florida, where he graduated early with a 4.0 average in civil engineering. This allowed him two seasons at Stanford under Coach Hornbrook. In this, his first season, Trip's game was blossoming.

At Florida, he had faced Heath Whitman twice, losing miserably the first time, 0-6, 1-6, and again the next year in the conference finals, 3-6, 4-6. Heath was a junior now, and the top player in college tennis. Trip knew this was going to be the match of his life.

Trip won the coin toss and elected to serve. Heath looked at the sun's position and chose a side, putting Trip looking into the sun for his first service game. Trip took his normal position for his first two serves, and Heath pounced on the returns, winning both points. Down love-30, Trip looked up at the sun and moved down the line to the far right—a normal service position for doubles play, but rarely for singles. This put the sun slightly out of his eyes, and he surprised Heath with a hard, wide serve for an ace. Moving to the other side, he moved along the baseline to reduce the sun's glare, lowered his toss slightly so he didn't look up as high, and put as much spin on the serve as he could. The slower pace and wicked bounce caused Heath to swing early and hit the return wide. The score was now 30-30. With renewed confidence, Trip again hit from the far side of the court, but placed it down the middle. Heath, expecting another wide serve, got to the ball late and hit it into the net. Trip won the next point to save his first service game.

Changing sides for the second game, Heath had similar trouble with the sun, but adjusted quickly and held his serve.

As the games progressed, Trip discovered the wisdom of his father's advice and Frank's coaching. For the new serve, Coach Hornbrook had changed Trip's starting footwork, his toss, his backswing, and his movement to the net as he hit the ball. Frank taught him to bend his knees more, giving him a spring action, then stretch toward a high service toss, causing Trip to come high off the ground and gain additional leverage.

For three months Trip had been running daily drills to develop the serve. He timed his wrist snap perfectly to increase his power and topspin, creating a massive kick that caused the ball to bounce high. The so called "kick serve" forced the receiver to take the ball high and out of their maximum power zone. As the match against Heath progressed, Trip knew his hard work was now paying off. His anxiety abated, his serve improved, and Heath began having trouble returning it. Trip was racking up service winners as well as short points when he put away Heath's weak return.

Now adjusted to the sun, both players held serve until the score in the first set was even at six games each. They played a tiebreaker, each trading serves until someone earned seven points. Each held his serve until Heath faltered, giving Trip a 6-5 advantage. Tournament play required that tiebreakers be won by two points, meaning that Trip needed one more point to win the game and the set. Trip noticed Heath take a half step toward the middle of the court, expecting Trip to go down the middle—his strongest and most consistent serve. Trip took a chance on an outside serve and hit the service line for an ace. He had finally won a set against the number one player in college tennis.

The second set went as the first, with Trip concentrating on his service game while waiting for a lapse in Heath's game and a chance to break his serve. Heath played flawlessly though, and again they went into a tiebreaker. Trip decided to gamble with a short drop shot return on Heath's first service. The ball grazed the top of the net with massive backspin causing it to bounce back toward the net and away from Heath, making for an almost impossible return. Early in the match, Heath would have probably gotten to the drop shot for an easy put-away, but now, after twenty-four games and into the second tiebreaker, his fatigue was showing and his reaction to the shot was slow. As with the first set, Trip won a service point from Heath and was up 6-5 and serving to win the match.

Trip saw Heath take a step to the outside, expecting the same serve as Trip had used to win the previous set. Trip went to his best serve down the middle and Heath had to leap for it, hitting it with little control. The ball sailed high, looking like it was going long, but the topspin generated by Heath's last second flick of the wrist caused it to drop slightly and Trip watched as it hit the back edge of the baseline just out of his reach for a winner. But the line judge called Heath's return "out," and the crowd erupted, cheering Trip.

Instead of celebrating, Trip immediately looked at the chair umpire expecting an overrule, but none came. Heath ran to the umpire's chair and went ballistic at the line judge's call.

Trip ran to the chair umpire as well. "Are you going to overrule that call?" he asked.

"I have to be absolutely positive to overrule, and it was too close for me to do that," the umpire replied.

"Well, it was clearly in, so overrule it," Trip said.

"Are you sure? The match is yours, Trip. Why are you questioning the call?"

"Because it was wrong! I want to win fair and square, not because a line judge makes a bad call," Trip argued as the crowd went silent, waiting for a verdict.

"Okay," the chair umpire shrugged. "The call is overruled," he announced. "Point goes to Mr. Whitman. Score is 6-6. Mr. Furman to serve."

The crowd stood in silent disbelief, then Mishael started waving her flag. Her entourage followed and they started chanting "Trip, Trip, Trip . . ."

Heath grinned and pumped his arms in celebration as Trip went to the baseline for his next serve. He noticed the line judge whose call had been overruled staring at him, furious. Trip had trouble regaining his focus. Heath took full advantage and pounded the return for a winner, putting him ahead by a point and giving him the chance to serve for the tiebreaker win and the set, which he did. The men were now tied at one set each in the best-of-three set match.

Trip regained his composure and his serve strengthened in the third set as Heath's stamina waned. On a return of serve, Trip hit a beautiful topspin backhand cross-court shot out of Heath's reach. The ball bounced off the baseline for the winner. Immediately the line judge called "out."

"What?" Trip yelled. "Are you kidding me? Are you blind?"

The line judge said nothing, but Trip detected a smirk. Trip ran to the chair umpire to question the call.

"Sorry, Trip," the umpire said. "That's across the court and I didn't have a good enough look to reverse the call."

"You're shitting me!" Trip yelled out of frustration.

"Careful, Mr. Furman," the umpire warned, dropping his informality to address the profanity. "I'll have to assess a penalty point if I hear any more from you."

Trip stood stoically, fuming, but said nothing else. He looked toward Heath who was snickering, glorying in his reprieve. As Trip walked back to the service line, he glared at the line judge with as much venom as he could muster. The line judge did his best to ignore the stare.

For the rest of the match, any close calls did not go in Trip's favor, and his focus was broken with each questionable call. The crowd started booing the calls and making so much noise during Heath's service games that the chair umpire stopped the match, threatening to clear the stadium if quiet wasn't restored. After a final loud hissing, the crowd quietened and play resumed.

At 4-4, Heath finally broke Trip's serve, and went on to serve for the match. Trip battled in the final game, fighting off two match points to stay even. But Heath's service game proved to be too much for Trip who finally faltered.

Heath came to the net for the obligatory handshake, and Trip steeled his anger as they met. Holding Heath's hand for a moment too long, he leaned toward Heath's ear and whispered, "I'm going to clean your clock next year, asshole."

Heath jerked back and just laughed—nervously.

CHAPTER 2

the locker room

Trip tried to contain his anger as the awards were presented, but he continually saw flashes of white as anger ripped through him. He felt betrayed and couldn't let it go. He had tried to do the right thing and be honorable. Instead, he was cheated by a vengeful line judge. Heath's mocking attitude at winning the championship just added fuel to the fire, and Trip could find no way to feign graciousness. The best he could do was go through the motions with his mouth closed, and get off the court as quickly as possible.

Finally, the ceremony ended and Trip grabbed his bag and headed for the locker room. His father, Joseph, was waiting for him.

Trip angrily threw his bag against the wall and started yelling. "That asshole line judge cost me the match! He stole it from me. And Whitman's just as big a cheat. He knew my ball was in! He should have said something!"

"Why?" Joseph said quietly, not responding to Trip's tantrum.

"Because he should have. He saw it. He knew!" Trip repeated.

"So what?" Joseph said.

"What do you mean, 'So what?'" Trip screamed. You saw it hit the line. You're not going to try to tell me the asshole line judge was right, are you? Come on, Dad! Whose side are you on?"

"Yours," Joseph calmly replied.

"Well, it doesn't sound like it!" Trip said as he leaned against the tile wall and slid to the floor in a hunched position, putting his head in his hands and shaking in disbelief.

"Trip, get up."

"I don't want to," Trip retorted.

"Get up now, I said," Joseph commanded, his voice loud and not to be ignored.

Trip had never disobeyed his father. He hesitated, wanting to tell his father to go to hell and leave him alone. But he didn't have the will to wantonly disobey. He slowly stood and glared down into his father's eyes. Although Joseph was several inches shorter than his son, his demeanor made him tower emotionally over Trip who cowered into submission.

Joseph was quiet for a moment, letting Trip regain composure, then asked, "Do you really think that just because you did the right thing, Heath should've?"

"But my shot was in!" Trip said.

"That's irrelevant," Joseph said. "Now answer my question."

"I don't know. I thought he would do the right thing. I thought he would overrule the call. It was a horrible call!" Trip stammered.

"Why? Because you did? Look son, just because you do what's right, you assume the world is going to do what's right. Don't be such a fool, Trip. Grow up and face the situation."

"I don't get you, Dad. You've always taught me to do what's right and now you're telling me I was wrong?"

"No. I'm telling you to grow up." Joseph paused as Trip just stared at him. "Let me say this first, before we get to the real issue." Joseph put his hands on Trip's shoulders and looked at him sternly. "I have never been more proud of you than when you went to the chair to correct the call. That was one of the best moments I've ever had on a tennis court. But for you to expect anyone else to behave like you is not only foolish, it's dangerous, as you found out."

"Dangerous? How's that? I don't get it," Trip said trying to figure out his father's simultaneous praise and admonishment.

"You think Heath was wrong not to question the call?" Joseph asked.

"Of course he was wrong."

"And, you think that because the line judge was wrong, and Heath was wrong, and the chair umpire was wrong, you had the match stolen from you?"

"Don't you?"

"Absolutely not!" Joseph said. "Who controls your head, Trip?"

"Me?" Trip said, knowing it was the wrong answer to give his father. When Joseph asked a question to teach a lesson, the obvious answer never seemed to be the right answer.

"It looked to me like Heath Whitman got control of your head today—with a little help from the line judge. But actually, you did all the work for him. And once he got control of your head, your match was lost. Heath not only didn't question a bad call, he rubbed your face in it. And in doing so, he beat you."

"So, are you saying I shouldn't have questioned my call?" Trip asked.

"You're way too smart to ask a stupid question like that, Trip. You questioning a call has nothing to do with the issue. The issue is your head, and who controls it. If you go into the pro ranks without total control, you're going to have your head handed to you on a platter. They have so many ways of tearing up your psyche, your head will be swimming before you've played two games. Never, ever let someone else's behavior dictate your attitude. You need to focus on Trip Furman, and who Trip Furman needs to be regardless of anyone else. Nobody is going to behave like you, and very few people even care. Heath didn't give a damn about you being a saint out there. He just used it to his advantage. That's all. That's reality. And that fact should have nothing to do with the way you feel about yourself, or what you should expect from him. Get it?"

"Yes, sir," Trip lamented. "I let my expectations get in the way of my game, and Heath used that and beat me. I shouldn't have expected anything better from him. He's just an opponent. I'm responsible for me and my behavior. I lost control of my focus."

"Now you're getting it, Trip." Joseph smiled.

"I hate it when you're right, Dad," Trip said. "Don't you ever get tired of being right all the time?"

Joseph grinned, marveling at his son. "I've been wrong far too many times to count, son. So, if I'm right occasionally, just let me enjoy it for a moment. I know that too will pass, and I'll be wrong again soon enough."

"I doubt it, Dad," Trip said. "Do you mind if I go now? I'm supposed to meet my date."

"No. You go ahead and have some fun. You've earned it," Joseph said.

"Thanks. I'll see you later?"

"Probably not. I'm heading back to Houston tonight. But I'll see you soon."

"Okay."

As Trip turned to leave, Joseph stopped him. "Trip?"

"Yeah, Dad?"

"Your tennis game is a beautiful thing to watch. Just beautiful."

"Thanks, Dad. I owe it all to you. See you soon."

"Say hello to that beautiful girl who was cheering for you so wildly. You'll have to introduce me to her sometime," Joseph said as he watched Trip pick up his bag and walk away.

Trip spoke over his shoulder. "Her name is Mishael. She's from Pakistan. A real, literal princess. And she plays the piano like you would never believe."

The locker room door opened as Trip was finishing his description of Mishael. His coach, Frank Hornbrook, came in smiling.

"What's up, Frank?" Joseph said as Frank grabbed Trip for a quick chest bump.

"Sorry about the match, Trip. We all know you beat Heath, but he got the trophy. Too bad, but the good news is, the athletic director just fired the line judge and the chair umpire. They'll never see another tennis match unless it's from the bleachers."

"A little poetic justice, I guess," Trip smiled. "Gotta go, Coach. Thanks again for a great season."

"Whoa there, Trip. I thought you'd be furious about the match. What gives?" Frank asked glancing at Joseph for a hint.

"I have Joseph Daniel Furman Junior for a father," Trip replied. "Life doesn't get any better than that, Coach. I'll get Heath next year, no problem. See you."

The door slammed behind him as Trip raced toward his apartment.

CHAPTER 3

mishael

Trip ran across the campus to his small apartment and quickly showered. He then crossed the street to the restaurant where Mishael's friends hung out.

"Anyone seen Mishael?" he asked before sitting to enjoy a beer.

"She went to the library," someone answered.

"Thanks," Trip said and left without ordering. Trip knew the library meant the eleventh floor of the library tower, at the end of the book stacks. He had met Mishael there a month before and had been immediately drawn to her.

They had talked for a long time, but she would not leave with him or agree to go on a date with him. She had told him to meet her and her friends at the Player's Retreat restaurant across the street from the library later, so he went early and waited for her. That evening and in every interaction since, Mishael had treated Trip like any other friend, and as much as he tried, he could never seem to get any alone time with her. She wouldn't separate herself from the crowd, and she refused his invitations to his apartment. At the Player's Retreat the first evening, Trip was forced to sit across from Mishael since her friends took the seats next to her. He leaned over and whispered, "Can we go somewhere else so we can talk?"

Mishael leaned back in her seat and shook her head.

Trip didn't take the hint. "I'd love to fix dinner for you. My apartment is close, and I'm not a bad cook, especially if you like seafood. I can't entice you away from here?"

Again, she shook her head, then responded, "I hear you play tennis."

Trip was encouraged as this meant she had inquired about him, so there was some interest.

"Yes," he said. "I play a little."

"A little?" she replied with a smirk. "You're the number one player for Stanford, ranked second in the country in college tennis, and it looks like you'll lead our team to the NCAA finals next month. Understating is an admirable quality, Trip, but I believe you've taken it to new lows."

"So, will you go out with me?" Trip pushed.

"No."

"Why? You don't like tennis?"

"Tennis is okay, and as much as I'd like you to cook for me, I cannot go out with you."

"Why?"

"I'm a music major. We spend more time practicing than athletes do. This is my one night away from the conservatory, so meet me here next week, same time."

"Can we go out after that?"

"No."

"I don't get it. Why not?"

"You'll never understand, Trip, but hopefully I'll see you here next week. And please don't ask me again to go out. The answer will always be no." She got up and left.

Before Trip could maneuver his way out of the jumble of tables and catch up to her, she had slipped out the door and was gone.

She was an enigma, and he couldn't get her out of his head.

• • •

The eleventh floor was empty except for Mishael, and she was waiting for him behind a row of books that offered privacy. To his surprise, she reached up and put her hands around his neck and kissed him so passionately he felt as if his heart would burst. His knees were weak at her touch and he slipped down to the floor against the wall and lifted her on top of him, returning her passion as if the world was ending. She didn't resist when he cupped his hand over her breast as she moved her body along his, gently stroking him until he was breathless with excitement.

He held her tightly and caught his breath enough to talk. "So, I take it you liked my tennis game?"

"It was okay," she whispered into his ear as she nibbled his earlobe.

"Okay?" Trip said, surprised. "With a reception like this, I figured you must have really enjoyed it even though I lost."

She sat up on him, her legs straddling his stomach, and caressed his chest. "This has nothing to do with tennis, my dear Trip. This has to do with you."

"I don't get it. What are you talking about?" Trip said, amazed by her passion, but puzzled that it had nothing to do with his tennis game.

"You didn't hesitate to question the bad call, even though it cost you the match," she said and bent down to trace his lips with her tongue.

As he tried to pull her close for more, she pushed herself up into a sitting position and flung her long black hair behind her head. Then she looked down into his eyes.

"Why did you question the call? You know your teammates are mad as hell that you cost them the championship. They think you're an idiot."

"Do you?" he asked.

"Does it appear to you that I think you're an idiot?"

"I guess not," he said and tried to pull her closer.

She stiffened her arms against his chest, preventing him from reaching her, but she began moving her hips against his belly, pleasuring herself and driving him crazy with desire.

"Oh, God," he murmured.

"Trip, have you ever been in love?"

He looked up at her, trying to think of an answer. "No. Well, yes. Lots of times. I mean like I've loved a lot of girls, but I don't know. What do you mean in love? Like in love enough to spend my life with someone? Like deeply in love? I don't think so, if that's what you mean."

Trip knew everything he was saying was wrong, but he couldn't stop talking. It was like when his father asked him a question, and he knew his answer would be wrong, but he couldn't help saying it anyway.

Mishael smiled at his fumbling, watching as he tried to squirm his way out of an answer. She bent down and kissed him to stop his talking, and as he responded, she sat up again and threw her hair back.

Trip marveled at her beauty. She was small, barely five feet tall he guessed, and slightly built. Her emerald green eyes and heavy dark eyelashes exuded an intensity that couldn't be ignored or forgotten, and were framed by her long, jet black hair and generous lips, so common among the people of the Mediterranean. The olive tone of her skin accentuated the only word he could think of to describe her—exotic. He was mesmerized by her and felt as if he was drowning in a quagmire of desire. He found it hard to focus his thoughts.

She whispered, "If you fell in love, do you think you'd know the exact moment you did?"

He looked up at her, his hands caressing her small waist and the base of her back as she moved slowly to his slight rhythmic thrusts. He didn't answer. Instead, he marveled. If he did answer, he would scream, "Yes!" And know that the moment was right now, and right here. Suddenly he felt like he never wanted to be without Mishael. What was it about her? He didn't know, but suddenly he knew he was in love like he never dreamed love could be.

Finally, he answered quietly. "I'm sure I would know the exact moment I fell in love."

"Me, too," she said. "I fell in love with you when you walked to the umpire's chair and did what was in your heart. You knew what was right and you did not hesitate. After that, I knew I could never love anyone but you, Trip. This is not about tennis. This is about you. I love you."

Trip started to respond, but she quickly covered his lips with her delicate fingers, quieting him.

"I don't want you to say anything right now, Trip. I don't want you to love me or say you love me because I said it. It's okay if you don't love me. I understand and expect nothing from you. But I have never seen anyone do what you did today. Everyone hesitates and weighs the consequences of doing the right thing—as if the cost of the action is more important than the action. I saw you today, Trip. I saw the man I thought I would never see. I will never see another like you, but I know that I fell in love at that moment, and the rest of the tennis match was irrelevant to me. I watched you after that—not tennis. Your passion overflowed in me, and I'll never be fulfilled by another man. I know you can't understand this because you don't know my family or my culture. But know this—if you stay or if you leave, I will not judge you any way but as the one love of my life. Do you understand?"

"No," Trip said, his voice barely audible. "I don't understand how you can see so clearly. I see you, and I see this moment. And I see that the moment I fell in love is right here and right now. I know that I never want to be without you. That is what I understand."

"I'm sorry, Trip, but you will have to understand much more than that or we cannot see each other," Mishael said.

Trip cut her off. "Of course we can. If we love each other we can be together forever. No one can come between us!"

"No, Trip. Listen to me carefully. You have no idea who I am or where I'm from."

"I don't care! I'll learn."

"Don't interrupt me, Trip. Hear me. We cannot be seen alone together. My family will not allow it."

Trip started to speak again, but Mishael put her fingers firmly over his mouth. "Listen. When we are in public, we must be in a crowd. Do not touch me or pay too much attention to me. We will be watched. Believe me. You may not call me, ever. I will leave notes for you here in a special book on the shelf. You can do the same and we can stay in touch that way. I'm going to leave a sealed envelope for you to open only if I've had to leave suddenly. I want you to do the same and leave me a final note, too. My final note is already there and sealed with my lips. Promise me you'll not open it."

"I promise," Trip said, confused by her motivation.

She continued, "Also, I practice in the conservatory at night. I must be out by midnight, or the consequences will be dire. When I leave, it will be by taxi which my parents send for me. There's a study hall in the conservatory near my piano. Start studying there, and when everyone leaves, we can be together. Wait for me to be gone a long time before you leave the conservatory. Do you understand?"

"I hear you," Trip said, "but I don't understand you."

"Then we cannot see each other again, ever. Do you understand that?"

"I can't bear that," Trip said. "I'll do what you say. One day things will change. I'll figure out a way for us to be together forever. I'll do whatever it takes."

"I know you will, my love. But it will be fruitless. I'm sorry. I have to go now. Come to the conservatory tomorrow evening around nine. Don't be early. Now you must stay here for a time so we are not seen leaving together. I love you."

She leaned down and kissed Trip, then quickly got up and left.

Trip lay on the library floor for a long time. He was both heartsick and overjoyed. His emotions were tearing him apart, and at the same time he had never been happier. *This is how far the East is from the West,* he thought. *It's like life is right in front of me, but an eternity away. I'll make sense of it tomorrow night, I'm sure.* He fell asleep dreaming of Mishael.

CHAPTER 4

the meltdown

Trip and Mishael established their routine and continued seeing each other surreptitiously during the summer, fall, and into the spring semester when he was again leading Stanford to a championship season. As much as Trip tried to get Mishael to relent and introduce him to her family and thereby, in his mind make it okay for them to date, she was adamant that her family never know about him.

One Saturday night as they lay together under her piano, she fell asleep in his arms and he watched as she breathed peacefully. He was so content to be with her. He marveled at her beauty as well as her playing, which was unlike any music he had heard. Sometimes, she confessed, she played her soul for him—and only him. This night, he too fell asleep, and did not awaken her in time for the taxi.

A door slamming woke them up.

Mishael sat up and looked around, getting her bearings, then panicked. "Oh, my God, Trip! What have you done?" Before Trip could react, she was out of his arms and adjusting her disheveled clothing.

"What's wrong, Mishael?"

Two men in black suits stood at the end of the piano, glaring at Trip. One of them grabbed Mishael's arm to pull her away.

"Don't you dare touch me. I'm Ameerah and when father hears you touched me he will have your head!"

The man stepped back, fear evident in his eyes. The other man spoke. "You missed your taxi. Your father is outside waiting. You must come with us." He cocked his head toward Trip. "Your father will deal with this infidel, I'm sure."

"Mishael, what's happening?" Trip screamed.

She didn't answer, but started for the door. He tried to catch her, but one of the men blocked his way, forcing him backward.

"Mishael! Wait!"

She turned to him, tears streaming. "Oh, Trip! What have you done! What have you done! My God! I'm afraid I'll never see you again! I have to go! Can't you see? You must let me go! Why didn't you wake me? I have to go!"

Trip tried to jump around the man to get to her, but was expertly blocked. "Mishael! You don't have to go. I'll protect you! I'll do whatever it takes! Don't go. Please don't go! I just don't understand. Why do you have to go like this?" He followed her to the door as the man stood between them and blocked the doorway after she left.

She ran, not looking back, and got into a black Mercedes.

Trip stood paralyzed, watching, not knowing what to do. He could see Mishael holding her head in her hands, sobbing, as the car sped away.

• • •

After walking around the campus in a daze, he decided to go to the library and wait until her first class the next day. Then they could talk and straighten everything out.

Impatience and fear overcame him, and he broke into a run to the library. He flung the doors open, waking the night guard, and ran to the elevators. When the elevator was too slow to open, he went to the stairs, running up them as his panic consumed him. Eleven flights and he couldn't get there fast enough. He nearly passed out

at the eleventh floor and literally crawled to the mailbox, unable to
get a breath. The books had been moved. His final letter to her in
the sealed envelope was gone as well as his last note, but there was
no reply note from her; just her sealed envelope. He ripped it open.
Her handwriting was beautiful, but what she wrote was devastating.

> *My dearest,*
>
> *If you are reading this and have honored our
> vow, then Father has discovered us and I am on my
> way home to an arranged marriage. I am helpless in
> preventing this, but please know that you are the love
> of my life and without you I cannot endure. Should
> I find a way to freedom, I will contact you with an
> ad for a 38-inch avocado oven in the Sunday edition
> of the Palo Alto paper. Call that number. If a man
> answers, hang up—I am gone and you are in grave
> danger. You must go on with your life, my love. I beg
> you not to wait for me.*
>
> *Please be careful as Father is a vengeful man
> and could have you followed for a long time. Please
> do not try to find me; it will be useless as well as
> dangerous. We were born into cultures which will
> keep us apart in this life, but I believe in my heart,
> we will be together forever as one.*
>
> *Know that I will die before I marry another. Pray
> that I have courage for that.*
>
> *I love you for eternity.*

Trip slid to the floor as his tears dropped on the note. He noticed
she used no names or places, so fearful was she that the note may
be found. He had never imagined the absolute control her father
exercised over her. Oh, that he had known and been as careful as she
had so often warned! How could he be so blind?

• • •

Trip skipped his classes to look for her, but found no sign of Mishael. Her friends had no idea where she had gone, or if they did, they wouldn't tell him. He went to the conservatory and found her locker cleaned out and her piano gone. Every morning after that fateful evening, he would go to the library to look for another note, but the book was always empty. He would find his note from the day before, remove it, and write another, hoping this one would find her. He didn't see her again.

A month later, as his tennis was suffering the effects of his losing Mishael, his father asked to meet him downtown. Coach Hornbrook had asked Joseph to talk to Trip and try to settle his spirit. Frank knew Stanford could win the championship if he could keep Trip focused, and he knew Joseph was the only one capable of getting Trip's head back in the game.

Joseph had mentored Trip his entire tennis career, and as a professional athletic scout and consultant to hundreds of coaches on the national arena, Joseph had handpicked the best coaches and programs for his son. Trip's attitude had been the focus of many discussions with his father over the years since it had surfaced at an early age while he was playing baseball. Joseph's discussions with his son had been attempts to allay the symptoms without addressing what Joseph was afraid was the real root of the problem. Trip showed symptoms of depression and Joseph feared Trip's melancholy had more to do with Trip's intelligence than with an emotional disorder, as it seemed to surface due to the monotony of developing the habits necessary for successful athletic mechanics.

Joseph had dealt with this issue on another occasion, when he had been called in to assess a professional golfer's lackluster performance after being the top collegiate golfer in the country. Sponsors had invested heavily in the golfer's career but were concerned and disappointed about the young star's poor play on the professional circuit. So, they asked Joseph to intervene.

Joseph asked to be informed when the golfer was practicing and watched from a discreet distance without drawing attention as the golfer hit his morning practice quota. Joseph had rarely seen more perfect mechanics and control, but what struck him was the golfer's demeanor. Although the shots were nearly perfect, they lacked fire. This was not something Joseph could see; it was something he felt. It was more about the way the golfer selected his club, initiated a practice swing, and teed the ball. His body was perfectly attuned to his task, but his brain was disengaged. Joseph ambled back to the group of sponsors' representatives gathered in the clubhouse where they anxiously awaited his assessment and expected a cure.

"Well, what do you think? Can you help him?" asked the Ping golf clubs rep. Joseph heard the impatient overtone of an instant-gratification junkie and decided to distance himself from this salesman. Joseph ignored the question and veered over to the table where coffee and bagels were set up, poured a cup of coffee, and sat near the Lambda Company salesman who had flown in from Europe in hopes of salvaging their investment. The persistent Ping salesman followed.

"Well?" insisted the Ping rep.

Again, Joseph did not acknowledge the question, but turned his attention to the group. Joseph asked if anyone could get the golfer's college transcripts.

"What the hell does that matter?" the Ping salesman demanded. "His grades have nothing to do with golf!" His impatience boiled over.

Joseph had had enough of the salesman and continued to ignore him. He raised his coffee cup to take a sip as he watched the rep's face redden. The tension was broken as two gentlemen entered the room. The golfer's agent was escorting a very well-dressed man, whom Joseph immediately recognized as the president of Ping North America. *They really did pull out the big guns for this,* Joseph thought as he watched the gentleman motion to his salesman to sit down and shut up. Then he nodded a respectful greeting to Joseph and moved through the crowd to shake his hand and pull him into a quick bearhug. The salesman, who immediately obeyed the president, looked around sheepishly, stung by the rebuke. He had not realized the regard Joseph commanded from these legends of the athletic world.

By now the Lambda representative had put his overstuffed briefcase on the table and was thumbing through a series of well-organized files. "We have a copy we can let you look at," the rep said as he pulled out a folder containing the transcript. He slid it across the table to Joseph.

"Thank you," Joseph acknowledged politely, as a stark contrast to the Ping rep's attitude. "You wouldn't happen to have his college golf scores in there, would you?" Joseph asked.

"Oh, yes," replied the Lambda rep. "Every tournament and every hole." He removed several large files and laid them out for Joseph.

"This may take a while," Joseph offered to the Ping president.

"I'm starving anyway and need breakfast, so take your time," he replied. Immediately a waiter was beside him with a menu, followed by a young girl with a silver place setting and a pot of coffee. Joseph was impressed. This club obviously knew how to cater to the wealthy. The Ping executive didn't take the menu, but quickly ordered. "Bring me steak filet rare, eggs and biscuits. Keep the orange juice cold and topped off. Eggs over medium." The waiter nodded, finished pouring him a cup of coffee, and left quickly.

Joseph spread out the transcripts and score sheets on the large table and started studying them. Thirty minutes later, as a busboy was clearing the breakfast dishes, the Ping executive sidled up behind him and politely enquired as to his progress.

Joseph pointed out their golfer was from Pinehurst, North Carolina, attended Duke University, majoring in physical science and applied mathematics, and graduated with a 4.0 average—not an easy feat at one of the premier universities in the country. And being from Pinehurst, he had grown up with a golf club in his hands.

"The significant aspect," Joseph showed them, "is his best scores came during the ends of the semesters, when exams were in full swing and term papers and project deadlines squeeze an athlete's mental capacity to an explosive pressure point. Your man thrived under this intensity. Now, with school removed, his brain is like a Ferrari with its twelve cylinders screaming at ten thousand RPMs, but going nowhere. In other words, he is bored shitless. Excuse the expression," Joseph quickly followed. "He is way too intelligent to just hit two hundred golf balls a day. I applaud him for trying, but he will never adequately focus on just a golf ball long enough to win tournaments."

"So, what do we do with him?" the golfer's agent asked nervously, knowing his large percentage of the winnings was in jeopardy.

"The best thing for him," Joseph replied, "would be for y'all to cancel his contracts and send him back to school so he can become a professor and a golf coach."

"Well, that ain't happening!" retorted the Ping salesman. The infuriated glance from his boss ended the man's rhetoric.

His goose is cooked, Joseph thought. *He'll be looking for a new job tomorrow.*

Joseph continued nonchalantly, as if the interruption had not occurred. "The best thing for *you* to do—and I'm not positive it will be successful—is to pull him from the tour for several months, give him a job as a researcher, and pay him to develop a new line of clubs. Have him keep practicing daily with the new club designs, analyzing them as he practices. Keep the pressure intense and put him back on the tour with new clubs, ostensibly to keep developing them as he plays. Keep his brain actively engaged in research and development while you promote his new products."

Few people in the industry were to know the result of this endeavor because it was impossible to deduce from the patents, but the oversized metal driver was born that year, as well as many other significant iron and shaft changes that revolutionized golf club designs for an entire generation. And very few people knew this successful golf pro was the brains behind the research and development that led this revolution. Joseph had admonished the group to keep it very quiet, as much for the benefit of their pro to not find out their strategy as for the industry to protect its secret investment. The manufacturing companies heeded his advice and guarded this knowledge as vigorously as Colonel Sanders guarded his famous fried chicken recipe.

A year later, after the pro went back on tour and won his first major, a package arrived at Joseph's Houston condo. In it was a series of thank you notes from each company represented in the clubhouse that day, and a bonus check from each, the largest being from Ping. His friend at Ping, whom he'd met in college competition and had kept in touch with over the years, orchestrated the response. Each company knew Joseph not only saved them a boatload of money, but also made them millions through the golfer's innovative products. It was a good day for Joseph, but at the time he could not have foreseen that his own son's dilemma would be so much harder to rectify.

• • •

Joseph never took the opportunity to tell Trip that his intelligence could become an overwhelming impediment to his career as a professional tennis player. He had hoped Trip would mature beyond the melancholy. Instead, Trip's melancholy seemed to metastasize as a demon in his soul. It was time to confront Trip.

Joseph pondered this meeting with his son. He knew it would not be like any other he'd had with him. Trip was now a young man on the precipice of his adult career and a mere pep talk would no longer be effective. He would have to deal with Trip as an adult and speak with him as an equal. He decided to engage Trip in a life story and let Trip draw his own conclusions and deal with his melancholy.

Joseph met Trip in the lobby of the hotel where he always stayed when he came to watch Trip's home matches.

"Trip, you want a drink?" Joseph asked as they found a private area to talk.

"No thanks, Dad. I really don't have a lot of time. What'd you want to see me about?"

A cocktail waitress approached them and asked Joseph, "Your usual, Mr. Furman?"

"Yes. Thank you, Amanda," he answered, handing her a tip. "That's for you. Put the drink on my tab."

"Thank you, Mr. Furman," she said as she turned toward the bar.

"She's cute, Dad. Does she always wait on you here?"

"She knows how I like my Arnold Palmers," Joseph replied.

"Meaning she knows how to turn it into a John Daly?" Trip quipped, anxious to get on with the meeting.

"You could say that," Joseph confessed with a smile, but was slow to start talking about the real issues. Instead, he engaged Trip in small talk about trivialities until his drink arrived. Curiously, Amanda did not bring it. A waiter who looked to be Middle Eastern brought it.

"He must be new here," he told Trip. "I've never seen him before. I wonder what happened to Amanda?" Trip paid no attention to the man. Joseph took a small sip and winced slightly, then began stirring the acrid drink with his straw as he began to engage Trip in a conversation.

Joseph took another sip and began. "Trip."

"What, Dad?" Trip snapped as his impatience with the small talk boiled over.

Joseph paused, then quietly asked, "Do you remember how many baseball games we won when I was coaching you?"

"A lot." Trip rolled his head back, knowing he was going to be stuck there for a while.

"No. I mean specific games. A real number with a real score."

"Well, Dad, I can probably look it up for you if you really need to know." The cattiness in Trip's voice built as he finished the sentence.

"What I really mean is, do you recall any single game score?"

"Not really, Dad. I don't much think about it."

"Exactly! Exactly what I meant. You know we played hundreds of games, and won a lot, like you say, but I don't remember any specific game, or win, or score. They just all run together into visions of seeing you hit, or field, or throw—little snippets of games, that's all. Except for one game. All those games, and all I remember is one inning in one game. And we lost. It was the best game of all my coaching."

By now some of Trip's impatience subsided. His dad was not one to reminisce and some, including his mom, considered him rather cold and calculating. But Trip felt he was getting a glimpse inside his dad, and curiosity began to replace his urge to run.

"You remember Coach Harvey?" Joseph asked.

"Yeah, Aaron's dad. Aaron was really good. Played college ball at Richmond."

"He was also Justin's dad." Joseph added.

"Oh, yeah. Poor Justin. His legs just wouldn't allow him to run. You remember what his condition was?"

"No, and that's not important now. He was a great kid with a great attitude and wanted to play ball like his brother in the worst way. I know it was hard for Chuck—Coach Harvey—to coach him after Aaron. But he did, and he did a great job with him."

"Didn't he always play first base?"

"Yeah. He didn't have to move too much there. But you know, even though he could play first, when it came to batting, he was a guaranteed out. Even if he hit the ball, he couldn't run to first, so he would move as fast as he could while the other team easily threw him out."

"I remember. I felt bad for him, but he always had a smile on his face," Trip remarked, wondering what his dad's point was.

"Everyone was watching him. I was watching Chuck. I guess it's a coach thing. I would watch the anguish. Not a bad anguish, but a loving anguish. There was tremendous love in that family, and it showed. I know I tell you what's wrong with youth baseball, and that's easy to do. But the Harveys were what was right with baseball. Anyway, the game I remember—well, actually the inning, or half inning—was against Coach Harvey. They were the home team, and we were ahead by one run going into the bottom of the last inning, so we had to hold them to win. They had runners on second and third with one out. You were playing shortstop, and Michael Carter was pitching. They were into the bottom of their lineup, and Michael struck out the next batter, so one more out and we would win."

"I get it, Dad. I know baseball."

Joseph paused at the interruption, and Trip saw the moisture in his dad's eyes.

Joseph continued. "Like me, Chuck liked to run the show from the third-base coach's box. But unlike me, he kept his scorebook with him. I saw him look at his book as Justin walked to the plate. My heart sank. Justin was the ninth batter. His number-one batter was on deck. Justin was a guaranteed out. Game over, unless Chuck subbed in a hitter, which I knew he could do. Chuck didn't flinch. Never gave any sign he was thinking about changing batters. He just watched his son make his way to home plate. All I wanted to do at that moment was signal Michael not to throw a strike. I absolutely did not want to win like this, and my heart was aching for Chuck. But I did nothing, and Chuck did nothing. He just watched his son swing the bat fruitlessly. Then an amazing thing happened. The ball hit the bat and it popped up behind first base. The second baseman ran for it, the right fielder ran for it, the first baseman backed up for it, and Michael stood on the mound like a statue. I watched as Justin walked as fast as he could, smiling, toward first while Coach Harvey was frantically waving his players from second and third toward home. The ball landed between our players, and the second baseman picked it up for the throw to first, but nobody was there. Except Justin, who was standing on the bag. Justin made it, the dugout erupted, and I tipped my hat to Chuck as he was running toward Justin to hug him. Greatest game I ever lost, son.

"Chuck was killed a year later. They put a plaque at the flagpole behind center field commemorating his service to our youth. But what I know is, he was the definition of integrity and what is great about many of our volunteers. He never made the headlines with crazy antics. He just served his kids faithfully and truthfully. Now I know, at your age, this story doesn't mean much to you. But maybe later in life, when winning becomes too important, you will remember Coach Harvey and realize life is more important than winning."

Joseph took another small sip and winced, then continued to stir the drink while he talked.

Trip sat quietly watching his father and hoping he would hurry and finish.

"Trip, I'm very sorry about Mishael. I know you loved her and I hope she returns soon. I know you're grieving, and I don't want to take that grieving away from you. It's vital and necessary, believe me. I went through hell when I lost my first wife and children. But I was given a second chance and you're part of that second family and I couldn't be more proud or happy. But sometimes you need to see the other players and consider them. Giving up tennis right now isn't going to bring Mishael back any sooner, so I encourage you to finish your season faithfully. Do that for Frank and then let's talk. If tennis isn't for you, then I'm okay with that. If you need time alone to grieve for Mishael, I'm okay with that, too. We can spend as much time as you need."

Trip didn't know how to leave his father, or what to say. He had never seen this emotional side of his dad, and he was uncomfortable. He stood and walked away.

What Trip didn't see was that Joseph sat for a while sipping his bitter drink, nostalgia catching up with him. For the first time in his life he felt his age. His son, whom he had late in life, was a man now, and beyond his control. His beautiful young second wife had moved on with men her own age, and Joseph could think of nothing more to do. *Maybe tomorrow will bring something for me,* he thought as he finished his drink. *Too much lemonade in this one,* he thought as the sour liquid left an acidic aftertaste. He got up and headed for the street where a taxi was waiting. As he exited the building, the door handle felt very heavy in his grasp. His knees buckled under him, and he fell against the glass. The floor was curiously warm and comforting, enveloping him as he closed his eyes for the last time.

· · ·

At odd times later in life Trip would remember this last conversation with his father. Sometimes he felt Joseph was sitting on his shoulder, reminding him. It was a scene he would never forget. All Trip ever knew was that after he left the meeting, Joseph remained to enjoy his drink. He never saw his father alive again.

Suddenly, Trip was left to finish his college career without his beloved Mishael or his adored father. Tennis didn't seem very important now, but he decided to finish the season for his teammates who still blamed him for losing the championship the year before.

Walking onto the court for the NCAA championship match, Trip could not shake his somber mood. This time last year he had led the Stanford tennis team to their first championship match and a chance to seal his number-one ranking in college tennis. Back then, Joseph was watching from his customary box on the first row with Frank, and Mishael was with her entourage cheering Trip to victory. Now, the two people he cared most about were gone and neither was there to cheer him on. He felt the futility of this match, not caring if he won or lost.

Trip could not give meaning to his efforts as he looked toward his father's empty box. A veil of melancholy engulfed him.

Trip looked up into the student section, even though he knew Mishael's traditional bleacher row was empty. Without her, her entourage would not be cheering for him. Sadness filled his heart and with massive effort, he steeled his emotions and put on his game face to start his final collegiate match.

Trip's strategy for the match was simple. He and his father had worked it out successfully last year when he faced this opponent, Heath Whitman. Trip, with the most powerful serve in college tennis, had not lost a service game this season and had set a record for the most consecutive service games won. If Trip could continue this pattern and win his service games here, then he would only need to break Heath's serve once in each set, and the championship would be secured. His father had encouraged him to be patient and conserve his energy, waiting for Heath to falter, then put all of his effort into winning that game. The strategy worked perfectly the previous year. Trip would use the same strategy today, and this time he vowed not to falter.

Trip pushed his melancholy into the recesses of his mind and gathered the mental fortitude necessary for his overpowering service. The first set went as planned. Trip poured on the heat, breaking Heath's serve. After that, he held the service break lead and won the set.

Trip was in a mechanical trance in the second set, and he broke early so he could cruise to victory just by winning his remaining service games. But now, with an NCAA championship riding on his final appearance, his demon of despair began insidiously gaining control over his psyche. At 5-4, he was serving for the title. He looked toward his father's empty box. *Was it empty?* He paused, blinked, then looked again. An overwhelming sense of futility, anguish, and anger engulfed him, and he cracked a routine forehand with his entire strength and no control. Three strings immediately popped on his racquet as the ball sailed into the upper deck. Trip slammed the racquet onto the court, crumpling it, and then walked over to the bench for a replacement. He could not regain his focus, and continually saw angry flashes of white instead of the tennis court. He lost his serve and the next two games to lose the set 5-7. Then he smashed another racquet against the player benches, forcing the chair umpire to admonish him for poor sportsmanship and assess a penalty point. The next set was a blur of blinding rage as Trip attacked every ball, crushing it without regard to control. He lost 0-6, smashed his last racquet, kicked his bag over the bench, then headed for the locker room. His emotional demon had finally reigned supreme. He did not return to the court for the presentation of his runner-up trophy, so Stanford graciously mailed it to his mother's house when he did not pick it up. He vowed to never pick up another tennis racquet.

CHAPTER 5

daniel

After the awards ceremony, Trip's coach, Frank Hornbrook, went into the locker room looking for him. He knew Trip missed his father immensely, and he also knew he had lost his girlfriend earlier in the semester under dubious circumstances. Apparently, she was someone whom Trip loved with the fervor of youth, and he was obviously having difficulty dealing with the situation. Frank had discussed the dilemma of Trip's emotional frailty with Joseph on several occasions, and as he searched for Trip he was formulating a strategy for dealing with the volcano that had finally erupted today on the tennis court. He wished Joseph were here now.

Joseph had always known what to do and always had the right words and demeanor to navigate through the raging storms that are part and parcel among the gifted, high-strung athletes who have the God-given talent to perform at the top echelons of their sports. But Joseph was gone, and the burden fell upon Frank to pick up the pieces of Trip and help this young man reassemble his life. It was not a task Frank was looking forward to, but for Joseph's sake, he would do his very best.

Frank found Trip huddled in a corner of the shower, fully dressed and sobbing. His long curly blond hair, now soaked from the water, hung limply around his shoulders and covered his bearded face. Frank turned off the steaming shower and slumped down beside the broken young athlete, quietly looking at him as his body convulsed with the racking sobs. *Such a gifted athlete,* Frank thought. *Perfect size and weight for any sport he wanted to pursue; reflexes second to none; eye-hand coordination the best I have ever coached; and as icing on the cake, a father who knew from the onset of his life how to develop athletic talent, and provided the very best coaching. This guy also is blessed with near-genius intelligence.*

For the first time in Frank's long and successful career as a coach, he felt totally inadequate to deal with this Adonis of human athleticism. Trip's tears subsided as the demon ran its course and faded into oblivion. Trip looked over at his coach through strands of unkempt hair, and started apologizing.

"Trip," Frank said softly, putting a hand on Trip's shoulder, "there's no need to apologize to me. I understand the pressure and the emotional roller coaster you've been on."

"I need to apologize!" Trip interjected. "To someone. To Dad, to everyone who has invested so much time into me for nothing! I'm a total failure. I'll never make it as an athlete. I just don't have it."

"Trip," Frank continued, "you are a great and gifted athlete who has just been through a pressure-cooker semester. Take a break and find your way. You can do it. I know you can."

"Coach, I saw my father in his box watching me, and then I blinked and he was gone. I couldn't stand it. First Mishael and then Dad. It all just hit me at that moment. I felt so alone, like nothing mattered at all. I wanted to kill. I've never felt such an urge to destroy. I was a human wrecking ball on a rampage. And all I really destroyed was my career. I'm done."

"Trip, you're the NCAA runner-up, and you're poised to break into the top circle of professional tennis. Your career is far from over. In fact, it's just beginning."

"No, Coach, I can't do it. I know I can't and I don't want to. I'm very sorry to have wasted your time, but I'm going to take a break, probably a permanent break."

"What are your plans?" Frank asked, surprised.

"Actually, I've been thinking about it since Dad's funeral. I don't think a tennis career is for me. I just can't get into it with the commitment it takes to play professionally. I think I'm going to talk to Dad's friend, Victor, about going to Houston."

"Houston? Are you sure that's what you want to do?"

"I'm sure." Trip hesitated. "At least sure enough not to jump onto the circuit right now. Maybe I'll take my time driving across the country and use the solitude to clear my head. I always solved problems better when I was alone and doing something mindless. Driving through the West seems pretty mindless."

"Is that your final decision? Nothing I can say?" Frank was picking at straws trying to find a way to settle Trip down and get him back on the court. He knew the young athlete would rocket to the top of the rankings if he started now.

"Yes. I really need the change. On so many levels." Trip said quietly.

Frank knew he was losing the battle and tried another approach. "That was quite a meltdown you had out there."

"I know," Trip paused in thought. "The emotions just engulfed me. I have to have a break."

"You know if you leave for very long, it will be very difficult to get your game back to this level."

"Yeah, you're probably right, but I really don't have it in me now. Probably never will. I don't have the drive and hunger it takes. Fortunately, I don't need the money and Houston is a good opportunity for me."

"Why Houston?" Frank knew the answer, but wanted to keep talking, hoping an opportunity to say something meaningful would present itself.

"Lots of reasons. It's not too close to Mom in Florida, and it's far away from Mishael's memories here, and Dad opened some opportunities for me there before he died. Weather's warm. God, I hate the cold. And I don't know anyone. Everything will be new. I've decided to go by my real name, Daniel."

"No more Trip, huh?" Frank felt like this was the final nail in the coffin. *Trip* Furman was a great tennis player. *Daniel* Furman was someone else altogether.

"Nope. This meltdown was Trip's last hurrah. Daniel will be a new man."

"I know I've said it before, but I'm really sorry about your dad. I miss him, too. He helped me a lot over the years, you know."

"Yeah, I've always seen his coaching philosophy coming out in you. You've been a great coach. Again, I'm sorry to disappoint you today." Trip was feeling like he wanted to end this chapter of his life, and looked for a way to wrap up the conversation.

"No need to apologize. I've been there, and I know the pressures and emotions of competition at this level. I'll only ask one thing." Frank paused, willing Trip to look at him, then continued. "If you decide to re-enter the game, call me first."

"I will, for sure."

"Okay, well," Frank spoke slowly, searching for meaningful words, but found himself at a dead end. He just finished with, "Keep in touch, Trip. Or should I call you Daniel now?"

"I think I'll always be Trip to you, Coach."

"I hope so." Frank said with finality.

The two quietly rose and hugged each other. Daniel grabbed a towel, shook his long hair out of his face while vigorously rubbing his head with the towel, and walked out of the locker room, his clothes still dripping.

Frank Hornbrook stood there for a while, wondering if there was any more he could have said to change Trip's mind, but he knew in his heart Trip was going to have to find his own way now, his own healing, and his own grace to face his demons. He turned off the lights and left.

CHAPTER 6

victor

After graduation, Daniel took a month to drive across the country toward Houston. It seemed a respite there might give him the time he needed to grieve. Victor had offered him a job, and Joseph had left Daniel a condo and a sports car, so the transition would be easy.

Daniel had heard his father talk about Victor occasionally, but until the funeral he'd never met him. Victor knew more about Joseph than anyone, including his mother, and shared many stories with Daniel as he grieved the night after his dad's funeral. Victor was easy to talk to and seemed genuinely interested in Daniel's well-being. He encouraged Daniel to visit him in Houston after graduation.

Victor was the sole head of a large conglomerate of companies he'd started after a short stint in the Marine Corps. He began his company with a small land development deal south of Houston that blossomed as NASA began a massive building campaign in an effort to eclipse the Russian space program. This construction provided a nearly limitless checkbook, and Victor seemed always to be at the critical juncture with the development resources to capitalize on this, as well as many other government-funded building initiatives. His parent company, VCM Investment & Management Associates, based in Houston, was the core of his international empire that spread its tentacles into every facet of the military/industrial building industry after its modest beginnings in private sector development.

At first, working for someone was not on Daniel's radar, so he dismissed the idea as he finished the semester. Daniel discovered that without his father's counsel, he was lost. But a month on the road was healing and a growth time for Daniel, and as he got closer to Houston, he decided Victor's offer just might be a good way to rejuvenate. At least it would give him something to do while he waited to hear from Mishael.

Daniel settled into Joseph's condo and after several days of cleaning and painting, he was antsy and ready to work. He awoke very early for his first day at VCM. He drove his father's old sports car downtown and almost missed the private garage where he'd been told to park. He braked quickly and heard tires screech behind him. A black Mercedes that had been behind him since he'd left the condo veered to avoid a collision. Daniel expected a hand gesture or at least a glare from the driver, but instead the driver looked away, avoiding eye contact. *Wow,* Daniel thought, *that's certainly different than Cali. Maybe I'll like Texas.* The parking attendant opened the gate for him, checked his ID, and gave him an access card with a number on it corresponding to his assigned space. *My own space,* he thought. *This is going to be a nice change from driving around Palo Alto looking for the rare empty space.* It was early enough that the building wasn't yet open to the public, so he had to knock on the tall glass doors to summon the night guard. Fortunately, his name was on the register so the guard let him in and escorted him to the elevators.

"Are there stairs nearby?" Daniel asked.

"Sure, but it's a long, hard climb. You're going to VCM, right?" the guard replied.

"Yep. It looks like I've got some time to kill, so if it's okay, I'll just take them."

"Suit yourself," the guard answered, pointing to a door at the far end of the lobby.

"Is there someplace to get a cup of coffee or tea?" Daniel asked.

"Café on the second floor. Should open in about fifteen minutes."

"Thanks," Daniel said as he headed toward the stairs. He found the small café and waited until it opened. He ordered hot tea and a bagel, and sat at a small table to enjoy it, then to the stairs, timing his climb to coincide with VCM's opening.

Sarah, Victor's personal assistant, met Daniel in the lobby and ushered him to his office, giving him pertinent information along the way. "We occupy three floors of this building, the third tallest in Houston. You're lucky, not many start out on this floor. You must have brought some nice clientele with you. You're young for that. I think you'll be the youngest associate on this floor. You'll have to go downstairs to rub elbows with your peers, but they'll probably have nothing to do with you since you're starting up here. Unfortunately, you'll also have a hard time breaking into the group on this floor."

"Why's that?" Daniel asked.

"They'll think you haven't spent your time in the trenches. It'll be hard to earn their respect."

"Okay. Can I move downstairs?"

"No. Victor insisted you be here. He doesn't make many mistakes or do anything lightly, so he must have his reasons. I know Victor and your dad were good friends. Where'd they meet?"

"They grew up together. He was at Dad's funeral. I met him there. I'd heard about him but had never met him. Does everyone here call him Victor? I've always referred to him that way because Dad did."

Daniel found he was at ease talking to Sarah, and she didn't seem to mind his inquisitiveness.

"Everyone. His number-one rule: We're all on a first-name basis here, even the PhDs. I think it keeps egos in check—and we have some massive egos here. But there's plenty of money to be made if you listen to Victor and follow his guidelines. He's really a remarkable man. You'll have fifteen minutes with him at ten-thirty. Don't be late, and don't be early."

"Don't be early?"

"Late is a waste of his time and disrespectful to him. Early is a waste of your time and disrespectful to yourself. You know the old military adage, 'Ten minutes early, you're on time; on time, you're late; ten minutes late, forget it?' He thinks it's bullshit—his term, sorry. If you can't manage your time, you're not smart enough to be here. Just be on time. I suggest using the stairs. The elevator will sometimes take a minute too long."

"I use stairs anyway. Rarely use an elevator."

"Except to get to your office, of course?"

"No, I used the stairs this morning."

"Forty floors?"

"Yes, six hundred sixty-four steps."

"You must be in very good shape," she responded incredulously.

"I try. I run five miles a day and arrived early this morning for the stair climbing."

"Where do you run?"

"Mostly around Lockwood Park."

"Really? Are you living in Lockwood?"

"My dad had a condo in Lockwood Towers I inherited. But only on the third floor, so not much of a climb for me there."

"My son, Jonathan, plays baseball at the youth league there, so maybe I'll see you around. Stop and watch a game sometime. You into baseball?"

"A bit. I played in high school."

"In Florida?" Sarah asked, revealing to Daniel she knew more about him than she let on.

"Yes. It's a pretty big sport there. I was actually scouted by Cincinnati and offered a scholarship to Maryland, but Mom wanted me to stay in Florida, and I really didn't want to pursue baseball, so I stayed in Gainesville for my undergrad work."

"That's great. We have a softball team that plays in the City League. I'll get them to recruit you."

"No, thanks." Daniel responded quietly.

"No? Why not? Is it beneath you?" Sarah mockingly raised her eyebrow as if to poke fun at Daniel.

"No, not at all. Sorry, I just don't play anymore. I prefer biking and hiking when I have the time. But I'd like to come watch a game or two. Where do they play?" Daniel asked, trying to hide his embarrassment.

Sarah grinned at his youthful awkwardness and let him off the hook with a polite answer. "Usually Lockwood Park, opposite side from the youth baseball field. That's twice you've apologized to me. You don't hear that word much around here. Victor doesn't like to hear it."

"So, he's out to alter my personality?"

Sarah was amused by the question. "He'll either celebrate it or destroy it, but listen to him." She paused and raised one eyebrow again, then, with a touch of sarcasm, added, "And make money."

"And that's twice you've mentioned making money. Is that all that's important here?"

"Ugh. Very *un*-politically correct question. But the real answer's no. As Victor'll tell you, life's most important, but once the money is made, quality of life's easier to achieve, although certainly not guaranteed. We've got a very high success rate for obtaining wealth, but not so high in achieving quality of life. Too many egos clashing. Victor's sent quite a few associates to New York—his idea of the gulag. And he's also very *un*-politically correct, so you may just get along with him."

They had been walking and talking, and Sarah paused at a set of glass doors.

"Anyway, this is your office studio—there are four associates, including you, and you all share Jennifer, your office assistant. She'll coordinate your appointments and handle the office and secretarial duties for you. By the way, her Christmas bonus comes exclusively from you and your studio associates. Victor gives nothing. There's a manual on your desk with company policies. I suggest you read it before your meeting with Victor. And Jennifer will probably already have some appointments for you this afternoon."

"Thank you. I guess I better start reading."

"Do you know how long it takes to get to Victor's office?" Sarah asked.

"Four minutes."

"You've done your homework," Sarah said in a manner that showed she was impressed.

"Only what I've learned I should do. It's what I don't know that scares me, but I'm good at asking questions. Even *un*-politically correct ones." Daniel smiled as he repeated Sarah's grammatical error.

Sarah caught the reference and smirked. "You'll do fine here. Buzz me if you need anything. Star two-fourteen is my direct line. See you."

"Bye, and thanks again." Daniel watched her for a moment too long as she walked away, her wavy, shoulder length brunette hair swaying elegantly with the rhythm of her hips. She looked to be about eight inches taller than Mishael. The painful thought of his lost love dampened his mood as he turned, walked through his studio, and looked into his new office. *Vanilla on a cake cone,* he thought. *I was hoping for something a bit more special, like Rocky Road. Oh, well.*

• • •

He sat at the large walnut desk and tried to focus on reading the manual. A new chapter of his life was beginning, and he wondered if he would ever again see his beloved Mishael.

At 10:25, the alarm on his Patek Philippe went off and Daniel closed the manual, picked up a note pad, put his fountain pen in his shirt pocket and headed to his meeting with Victor. The watch and pen had been his father's—presents from Victor. Daniel wondered if Victor would notice he now used them.

Precisely at ten thirty, Sarah tapped her intercom and told Victor Daniel was waiting. The reply was immediate, and Sarah motioned Daniel to the large double doors of Victor's office. Victor rose from the leather sofa and met Daniel as he came toward him, his hand outstretched for a firm handshake and a congenial pat on the back.

"Welcome to VCM," Victor said. "Have a seat." Victor pointed to a plush leather chair adjacent to the couch, and returned to his place on the sofa.

As Daniel was taking his seat, Victor's valet offered him a cup of hot tea.

"No, thank you," Daniel said, unsure of whether or not he should be casual enough to enjoy tea in a business meeting with Victor.

Victor, sensing Daniel's anxiety, said, "Try the tea, Daniel. I think you'll like it. I have it imported from a small village in southern China. It's really a remarkable variety, and I know how much you enjoy a good cup of tea. Try it without sugar first, then if you still want a little sweetener, Robert will put a bit of muscovado from Barbados in it." Robert refilled Victor's coffee while Daniel tried the tea.

"It's perfect, sir," Daniel said. "I think I'll forego the—" Daniel paused, trying to remember what Victor called the dark brown crystals.

"It's just brown sugar," Victor chimed in, "but in Barbados, they know just how much molasses to leave in. It's called muscovado."

"Yes, thank you. The tea is excellent just as it is." Daniel now assumed this meeting was more of an initiation into VCM than an actual business meeting, so he put his pad on the low walnut coffee table, and sat back to enjoy the tea. He waited for Victor to open the conversation.

Victor waited until Robert left the room and then asked, "How is your first day going? You like your office?"

"It's great. So far, I've just been reading the manual, so it's been quiet. It's nice having my own parking space, too. I almost caused an accident getting into the garage, though. It cropped up on me rather quickly."

"You're driving Joseph's Porsche?" Victor asked, more as a statement than a question, so Daniel assumed he knew the answer.

"Yes, sir."

"It's a quick little car. I hope the other driver wasn't upset with you," Victor said, grinning.

"No," Daniel said. "Quite the opposite, actually. They had been behind me all the way from the condo, and swerved to miss rear-ending me, then passed as if nothing had happened. Didn't even look my way, although I tried to wave an apology."

"Curious," Victor said. "Well, let's go over some projects and prospects I'd like you to start working on."

With that, the pleasantries were done and the meeting turned into the business affair Daniel expected. As they were reviewing business, Victor would occasionally turn to his laptop for messages and information, but the meeting never seemed to be jeopardized by the interruptions.

Victor ended the meeting and walked Daniel to the door, shaking his hand again as he left. Sarah was talking to Victor's next appointment, so Daniel exited the office without speaking to her as he had hoped to do.

As Daniel left, Sarah ushered Victor's next appointment, Jeffrey, one of Daniel's studio mates. Victor had summoned Jeffrey while meeting with Daniel.

"Good morning, Jeffrey," Victor said.

"Morning, sir," Jeffrey responded.

Victor got right to the point. "I want you to find out who followed Daniel this morning. They almost rear-ended him at the entrance to the garage. Also, put a tracker on the Porsche."

"I heard Daniel talking to a mechanic this morning. It seems his old Honda is having troubles after the trip across country. That must be why he's driving the Porsche. You want me to track the Honda also? I can put a device on it while it's in the shop." Jeffrey said.

Victor thought a moment. "What if you arrange another car for Daniel? Maybe he'll need a replacement for the Honda. I'd like to see if we can get the tail to follow us. Think you can do that?"

"I'll figure something out, sir."

"Thanks, Jeffrey. Keep me informed," Victor said as Jeffrey left his office.

CHAPTER 7

eric

"What the hell? Jennifer! Get in here!"

"Yes?" Jennifer answered meekly.

"Get in here and close the damn door!"

Daniel walked out of his office and looked around. A muted voice harangued from Eric's closed door.

"Don't mind Eric. Hello. You must be Daniel?"

Daniel turned to see a dark, bald head leaning out of a doorway. "What's that all about?" asked Daniel.

"Just Eric's daily blast. Mostly I think he invents something to give her hell about."

"What's his issue?" Daniel asked.

"Probably didn't get his way about something and blames her. I'm Jeffrey."

"Hi, Jeffrey. Daniel."

"Welcome to VCM."

"Thanks. I think I saw you as I was leaving Victor's office? You were meeting with him after me?"

"Yep, you slipped out before Sarah could introduce us." Jeffrey said.

"Sorry. Y'all looked busy, so I didn't want to interrupt."

"Oh, that would have been okay, but I appreciate the consideration. Victor said you almost had a little fender bender this morning."

"He told you about that?" Daniel said, surprised Victor had paid any attention to the small talk.

"He just mentioned it and wanted me to ask about it in case we need to make our entrance to the building a bit more noticeable. You'll find he's very detail oriented."

"Wow. I guess so. It seemed like nothing to me. The car had just been following me since the condo and I guess the driver wasn't expecting me to turn so quickly. I really didn't think it was a big deal. The guy acted like nothing happened. I mentioned it to Victor just as a way to make conversation, not to make an issue of it."

"Yours is the red Porsche?" Jeffrey asked.

"Yes."

"Nice. How many miles on it?"

"Fairly low, considering its age." Daniel was delighted Jeffrey was interested in cars. "Dad left it to me along with the condo."

"That's probably one you should keep garaged and not use as a commuter. It's in beautiful shape."

"You're probably right, but it's all I have at the moment. I'm afraid the trip across the country was my old Honda's final hurrah. I took it in to get some repairs done, and the mechanic just called with an estimate that's a lot more than the car is worth, so I guess I'll be driving the Porsche for a while."

"Hey, you know Charlie in purchasing has been trying to unload his BMW. He lost his license for speeding—again. He'll let the BMW go cheap, and it's in great shape. Parked downstairs, too. Why don't you try it out? I'll call him if you want."

"Sure," Daniel said. "It's worth a shot, I guess."

"You going to Dallas tomorrow?" Jeffrey asked, changing the subject.

"Yes."

"Me, too. You want a ride to the airport?"

"Airport? I was going to drive. I didn't think about flying. Seems expensive just to go to Dallas."

"Boy, you are green. We fly here. Get Jennifer to get you the airplane schedule. Try to keep your out-of-town appointments in line with the planes. Jennifer's good at that. No doubt that's why your Dallas appointment is tomorrow. Second floor has one airplane. Beautiful Grumman Gulfstream. Third floor has two jets. Victor has his own, of course. But if there's room, you can book on any. Seniority rules, though. Jennifer will handle it. Tell you what, I'll get the keys from Charlie and you drive the BMW home tonight. I'll take the Porsche if you want. Then I can come by the condo in the morning and we can drive in together. I'll be there at seven and walk you through the paces. Later." Jeffrey left as quickly as he had appeared.

• • •

Eric's rant had run its course, and Jennifer opened the door, exiting with tears. Daniel looked away so as not to embarrass her.

"Jennifer?"

"Yes, Daniel?"

"Am I supposed to drive or fly to Dallas tomorrow?"

"Oh, yeah. I was just about to go over the plane schedule with you when Eric called. You'll fly. Plane leaves at nine. Be at the tarmac at eight fifty-five."

"Isn't that cutting it close?" Daniel asked.

"This isn't the airlines; you'll get used to it." Daniel detected an edginess to Jennifer's voice.

"Jeffrey offered to pick me up at seven o'clock and take me there."

"Oh, you talked with him? He already told you you're flying?" A touch of surprise in her voice.

"Well, he said you'd go over it with me. I thought I was driving, so he figured you hadn't had time yet to tell me details. He offered to walk me through my first trip. I didn't mean to sound critical that you hadn't told me yet. I guess I should've been a bit patient and waited for you to tell me details."

"Never mind," Jennifer said. "I'm always a little testy this time of day. Let's go to the conference room. I'll go over things with you."

"I can pull up a chair here and we can go over it."

"No way. Eric insists conferences occur in the conference room. We've already spent too much time here."

"Even for something as informal as this?"

"Especially for this. Come on."

"Jennifer, do you know anything about a guy in purchasing named Charlie?"

"Everybody knows Charlie. Why?"

"Jeffrey said he has a BMW for sale I should look at. I think my old Honda is dead. What do you think?"

"Charlie's always got a fast car somewhere, but he also has a lead foot," Jennifer said, her attitude lightening. "If he took care of his family and his foot like he takes care of his cars, he'd still be married to his first wife and have a driver's license. I'm sure the car will be in perfect condition. You should consider it."

"Thanks. Jeffrey's getting the keys so I can try it out tonight."

"Jeffrey's a good guy. Stay close to him and as far as possible from Eric. Just saying."

Jennifer closed the conference room door and started going over company details with Daniel. She was very patient, and very thorough. Daniel felt like he had found a second mom in Jennifer. He couldn't understand why Eric would harangue her so unmercifully.

As soon as Jeffrey was out of Daniel's sight, he called Victor. "Sarah, is Victor available?"

"He's on his way to lunch, Jeffrey. Hold on, I'll transfer you to his cell phone."

Jeffrey heard some clicks on the phone, then Victor answered.

"Hi Jeffrey. How'd it go?"

"He's driving Charlie's BMW home, and we can take the Porsche."

"Good. Maybe we'll be able to find out if he brought any baggage from Palo Alto. Any information on the Mercedes?"

"It's leased to a company in Arizona. We'll set up a traffic stop if it follows the Porsche, and we'll get some info on the driver."

"Great. Let me know as soon as Daniel leaves and we'll leave right after."

"Got it. Bye." Jeffrey said.

"Jeffrey?"

"Yes, sir?"

"Keep a close eye on him until we know something."

"I will, sir. I'll be picking him up in the morning and flying with him to Dallas. Jennifer will keep our schedules tight. He won't suspect I'm watching him," Jeffrey said.

"Watch your back on the way to the airport."

"Don't worry. I'll lose any tail we have going to the airport and let you know of anything out of the ordinary."

"I worry, Jeffrey, but I know he's in capable hands. Do you have enough work to keep you occupied?"

"Plenty, sir. With the Russians and Chinese at each other's doorsteps, I'm kept very busy these days. But I won't take my eye off the kid."

"Thanks, Jeffrey. By the way, that was a great idea to contact his mechanic and have his car deemed unfixable. He'll like the BMW better, anyway."

"I'm sure he will." Jeffrey said.

"Make sure the mechanic keeps the Honda, and tell Charlie to make Daniel an offer that's too sweet to refuse."

"Will do, si—" Jeffrey heard Victor's phone go dead before he finished his answer. Victor wasn't one to waste time on pleasantries.

jonathan

"DANIEL!"

Daniel squeezed the brakes and turned his bike in the direction of the shouting. He looked up to see Sarah waving at him from the bleachers of the Lockwood Youth Baseball Field. He waved, parked his bike and climbed up the framework of the bleachers toward her.

"So, you run in the morning, bike after work, and climb like a monkey?" Sarah asked as Daniel joined her in the seats.

"When I get home early enough. Is Jonathan playing?"

"He just finished his two innings. Struck out his one time at bat, but he tries hard. I wish I could help him, but I'm worthless at baseball." Sarah flashed a cute frown.

"Is his father helpful?" Daniel asked as he watched the teams change places on the field. He tried to pick out Jonathan as they disappeared into the dugout.

"Are you kidding? He's just plain worthless. Left when Jonathan was three and hasn't returned. I'm not even sure where he is now."

"But you wear your wedding rings?"

"We're not divorced. Plus, they keep away the cheesy come-ons. Jonathan is enough of a responsibility for me right now."

Daniel looked away as he heard a coach yelling at his players. "That sounds like Eric! What's he doing here?"

"Oh, he coaches the other team. They're in first place. Of course, he stacks his team. But winning never seems to be enough."

"He's yelling at his players?" Daniel said incredulously.

"Mostly his son. Like I said, winning isn't good enough. His son missed a play—over-threw first and allowed a run to score. Eric went ballistic. How's work going? I see your studio-mates haven't run you out yet."

"Jeffrey's been pretty nice. We flew to Dallas last week, so we got to talk a little. He's showing me the ropes. I'm sure he doesn't want to let on he's helping me. It's obvious Eric wants me to crash and burn, and Marlene just minds her own business and stays out of our way. At least she introduced herself. Eric acts like I don't exist, which is fine with me right now. I've got a lot to do and a whole lot to learn. I picked up a contract on a building this week. I'm working through the due-diligence now."

"Really? That's great! Where's the building?"

"Downtown."

"Oh? Which one?"

"It's called the Hudson. It's at—"

"I know where it is. I'm fairly familiar with it. Does Eric know you got that contract?"

"I don't know. Why?"

"He's been after that for a year. He's going to be pissed when he finds out."

"God, is he berating his kid over there again? That's horrible. Why does the league put up with that?" Daniel's agitation was growing as he watched Eric's antics.

"Technically, they don't. He's been warned, but he wins, so the parents look the other way. Nobody's going to say anything as long as he's winning."

"Winning? I thought this was youth baseball. What about the kids? He's everything you don't want in a coach!"

"Hey, you're preaching to the choir here, but I stay out of his way. I'm glad he didn't want Jonathan. Not that Jonathan's coach is very good. He's apparently a history teacher at the high school who doesn't know too much about baseball. But he's nice and tries hard enough and gives the kids their playing time." They watched quietly as Eric's team made the third out. "Looks like the game's over. Slaughter rule," Sarah said as she stood up and started down the bleachers.

Daniel followed. "It looks like they're having fun now." He watched as the kids grabbed their snacks and started a game of tag with the coach trying to corral them for a little end of game pep talk. In left field, Eric's team was in perfect order, and Daniel surmised he was going over every play and hit, and emphasizing each error, as bad coaches are apt to do.

"I think he could use some help," Sarah said, pointing to Jonathan's coach. Daniel didn't respond as he watched Eric, remembering the one year he played when his mom's boyfriend coached.

Back then, the rides home were always miserable. His mom's boyfriend, who required that Daniel call him "Dad," chastised him for his errors. Daniel might have pursued baseball had this jerk not taken all the fun away. "Dad" saw himself as an expert, but Daniel saw him as just a Monday morning quarterback who could tell you what you should have done, but never showing how or offering encouragement. Fortunately, Daniel's mom dumped him after the fight they had about Daniel quitting baseball.

"Daniel?" Sarah prodded.

"Oh, sorry. I was watching Eric."

Sarah looked out toward Eric's team and shook her head. "All those kids want to do is get their snacks, but Eric loves listening to himself. Tomorrow they'll be carrying concrete blocks."

"What?" Daniel gasped.

"Oh yeah. For every run the other team scores, the players have to carry a concrete block around the bases, and for every error made, another lap for that player."

"You've got to be kidding! That's insane! How does he do in post-season?"

"Terrible," Sarah said. "He's never made it out of the districts. The only reason he wins here is because he stacks his team and then insists on taking them to the tournaments."

"Figures," Daniel said. "Nobody ever improved their game carrying concrete blocks. Practice and good coaching are the only ways to reduce errors. I guess he doesn't really know what to do, so he just massages his ego instead. The more I see of him, the more massive his ego seems."

"Victor tends to disagree."

"Really?" Daniel said. "That's curious, since it seems to be so obvious. You seem to know a lot about what Victor thinks."

"Just comes with being a personal assistant. I get to listen to many of his conferences and write all of his lectures, so I do get immersed in his thoughts."

"Must be very interesting," Daniel mused.

"I enjoy it. It can get hectic and stressful, but he knows how to keep perspective."

"So why did he put me on the second floor? I'm still puzzled. First-floor associates look at me with darts. Some really do seem to be more deserving."

"I'm sure he had his reasons, but that's not something I would discuss, even if I knew. You're still not shy with questions, are you?" Sarah cocked her head.

"Bad habit, I guess. Always looking for info. As I said, what I don't know scares me."

"The only thing I can tell you is he likes to let the best learn to swim in the deep end, so he must see something in you. Or maybe your dad twisted his arm."

"How can that be? I didn't meet him until after Dad was gone." Daniel said.

"Don't kid yourself, Daniel. Victor has known you your whole life. Your dad and Victor spent more time together than anybody realized."

Daniel sensed Sarah knew more about him than she admitted. "So why did Dad never introduce us?"

"Probably had more to do with you living with your mom than it did with your dad," Sarah said. "Also, you've had your own life for a long time now. But your dad was always moving in the background. He just never told you."

"Did you know Dad well?" Daniel asked, trying to draw more information from her and probe the depth of what she knew about him and Joseph.

"Well enough, but only through Victor. They were both so competitive, but they channeled it way differently. Being in the room with both of them was electric. Victor misses him terribly."

"When will I get another fifteen minutes?" Daniel asked. "I haven't heard anything from him since our meeting. No feedback, no anything. Is that normal?"

"He's very busy, but keeps tabs on everything, including you, I'm sure," Sarah said. "As long as you're on the right path, you probably won't hear much from him. Looks like the kids are through with snacks . . . Jonathan! Jonathan! Over here!"

Jonathan came up, smiling, with the remains of devil's food cake and icing still on his teeth and lips.

"Say hello to Mr. Daniel Furman," Sarah said.

Daniel put out his hand to Jonathan. Jonathan shyly put out his hand. Daniel reached out and took it and shook. He noticed it was limp and unsure.

"Hi, Jonathan. How's the baseball?"

"Fine, I guess. I only play two innings and bat once. I strike out mostly."

"The important thing is you're playing. Are you having fun?"

"Yeah," Jonathan said, impatient to get back to his friends.

"Yes, *sir*, Jonathan," Sarah piped, correcting Jonathan's manners.

"Yes, sir. My best friend plays third base, so we have fun, but it'd be more fun if I could hit the ball."

"Is that your bat?" Daniel asked.

"Yeah. I mean, yes, sir," Jonathan corrected after he caught Sarah's stern look. "My friend Steve gave it to me. He got a new one this year."

"Can I see it?" Daniel asked.

Jonathan handed him the bat. Daniel held it for a moment, then handed it back.

"Can you swing it for me?"

Sarah stepped back, watching curiously. Jonathan took a swing.

"No, I mean stand and swing it like you're up to bat," Daniel said.

Jonathan stood still for a moment and swung the bat again. Daniel was quiet for a moment, searching for something encouraging to say, but instead changed the subject.

"What position do you play?" Daniel asked.

"Right field. Can I go now, Mom? Steve's waiting."

"Okay. I'll pick you up after pizza. Be good," Sarah said.

"See you, Jonathan," Daniel said.

"Bye," he said, running off.

"Well, what do you think? Can you help him?"

"You're pretty direct. What makes you think I can help?"

"You wouldn't have held his bat or asked him to swing if you couldn't help. So, what do you think?"

"Honestly?" Daniel asked, unsure if he should tell Sarah how bad Jonathan's swing was.

"Why bother with anything else? I'm his mom and under no illusions about his ability. Spit it out. Obviously, you didn't like what you saw."

Daniel decided it was best not to gloss over the issue, so he launched directly into a critique. "His bat is too big. It needs to be two inches shorter with a smaller grip. His grip is wrong. His wrist is cocked wrong; his elbow is raised, probably because the only instruction he's gotten from his coach is 'Raise your elbow.' You hear it all the time in youth baseball. Horrible instructions, but for some reason it won't die. His stance is bad, he can't shift his weight, and he closes his eyes when he swings. He's doomed to strike out, and if he accidentally hits the ball, it will be lucky to get back to the pitcher."

"Wow. That lays it out. Is that all? Rhetorical. I don't want to know if it isn't. How did you get all that in thirty seconds?"

"It's not hard. The trick is to know what's right."

"What do you mean?" Sarah asked.

Daniel continued explaining what his father had taught him. "Dad never spent more than five minutes assessing a player. And he was rarely wrong. It would piss off coaches who would encourage him to keep watching. But it's like looking at counterfeit money: there are a thousand ways to do it wrong, but only one way to do it right. And you don't bother learning the thousand ways, or even look for them, just as a money inspector doesn't study counterfeit bills. He studies the real thing, and studies and studies and studies, so his brain is so attuned to the right that the wrong is immediately and flagrantly obvious. Successful athletes have extremely similar mechanics fitted to different bodies, but still, very similar mechanics."

"So why do the big-league batters have such crazy stances and pick up their legs and put on such a show when they're batting?" Sarah asked.

"Look at them the moment they hit the ball. All the show beforehand is to get them to that moment. It's the only moment that matters. Plus, they are very consistent with it and have done it ten thousand times. But the critical moment is very similar, different only due to body differences, not mechanical vagaries."

"Apparently then," Sarah said, "you know what to look for. But can, or more importantly, *will* you help him? I hate to be so forward, but a single mom doesn't have time to dance around a subject. I understand if you can't, but I have to ask."

"I can help some," Daniel said. "I can't make a slugger out of him, but if he got just one hit this year, it might be one of those life memories for him—if he wants it and will work. Also, there's no substitute for practice and drills. He can't practice without me watching. He has to get it right so many times his muscles won't allow him to do it wrong. Practicing right one time with me and wrong ten times by himself kills everything. I really doubt we'll have time for that, though."

"The Baseball Nazi, huh?" Sarah said as she raised one eyebrow. "Is there fun built into this program anywhere?"

"Ugh," Daniel shrugged. "Okay, you nailed me. But I do understand the fun aspect, especially at this age. I will tell you this. Hitting a baseball is incredibly fun. When everything comes together and you feel the bat connect, there's just nothing like it. I think it's one of life's great mysteries. There's just no explanation for the simple act of swinging a bat and hitting a ball and feeling like the whole world is perfect for one instant. Striking out is not fun. Worrying about striking out is devastating. Walking up to face a pitcher, knowing you can hit anything he throws at you changes everything. So, I promise to make it fun for Jonathan, but he has to be willing. I can't do that for him. And sorry, but I don't have a lot of time to spend with him."

"I understand. Fair enough," Sarah said, then asked, "When do we start?"

"Where's a batting cage?" Daniel said, looking around the complex.

"The best one is over at the big field, but it's rarely open. There's an old one behind the T-ball field, but I don't know if it's usable."

"Okay. I'll find it. Can you meet me there tomorrow morning?"

"We go to church," Sarah said.

"Early service?"

"We can."

"Meet me at ten-thirty, then?"

"We can do that," Sarah said. "What should I bring? Do I need to get him a new bat?"

"Don't bring anything. I'll have it. See you then?"

"Absolutely. This is great, Daniel. I can't thank you enough. You just don't know how much this means to me."

"I haven't done anything yet. Thank me *if* he gets a hit this year. I'll go check out the cage. Oh, give me your hand."

"What?" Sarah said, again raising her eyebrow.

"Just shake my hand," Daniel said, trying not to be distracted by her facial expression.

"Okay?" Sarah hesitated, eyeing Daniel.

"Look," Daniel said, now wishing he hadn't started this. "Just teach Jonathan how to shake hands. Players begin and end competitions with a handshake and it's a small thing but incredibly important, like body language to a poker player." Daniel showed her the 'v' at her thumb and index finger and how to grasp firmly and positively, never looking down while shaking hands. "Since you don't shake your own son's hand, you probably haven't picked up on it, but Jonathan needs this. It's a first step in a relationship, and even if it doesn't make him the top dog, at least he won't be made out to be a wimp. There's a lot of psychology in athletics, so he needs to start early establishing dominance."

"Whatever," Sarah conceded.

"Just trust me. See you tomorrow." Daniel turned to get back on his bike as Sarah touched his shoulder.

"Oh, yeah. Before you go. Victor asked me to ask you about the Westmoreland Country Club."

"What about it?" Daniel asked as he secured the pedal clips.

"Are you going to keep your dad's membership? Most of the associates have a membership there."

"I know I inherited the membership with the condo, but I haven't decided whether or not I'm going to keep it. I checked it out. The pool is nice, but I don't play golf, polo, or croquet. A little tongue-in-cheek with the croquet; I think you have to be over sixty-five to get near the game," Daniel smirked.

Sarah put on a sales voice. "The pool is good, the food is great, they have some good bands on weekends, and the best clay tennis courts in the city; and one grass court, believe it or not. And the croquet is serious, mind you."

"I'm sure it is," Daniel laughed, then with a touch of seriousness, added. "I heard about the grass court. But at $125 an hour, I doubt I'll ever walk onto it. Are you a member?"

Sarah's sales bravado simmered. "Yes, Victor bought a membership for me. One of the only extras I've ever gotten, and he pays the monthly base fee. I have to pay for food and other stuff, but it's really nice. I get a spa treatment while Jonathan plays in the chess tournament once a month. It's heavenly." She ended on an upbeat note.

"All right. I'll think about it. Later." Daniel clipped his shoes into the pedals as he took off on the bike.

Sarah watched as he rode off with his hands crossed over his chest. She watched as the bike bumped slightly crossing the entrance to the parking lot; still, he didn't grasp the handlebars. *Showoff!* she thought, smiling. *Or maybe it's just his natural confidence. Wonder what Victor would say?*

CHAPTER 9

jonathan's tutelage

"Where'd you get the lawnmower?" Sarah called out to Daniel as she pulled on Jonathan's arm, willing him to walk faster to the batting cage. Sarah knew Jonathan wasn't enthralled with this idea. He accused her of just wanting a date with this guy and told her he wasn't looking forward to putting up with a man in her life.

"Found it on a trash pile," Daniel replied.

"You're dumpster diving?" Sarah asked with a facetious grin. "I thought VCM paid you at least enough to live on."

Daniel laughed, enjoying Sarah's easy ribbing. "Old habit," he replied. "I used to find all kinds of trash treasure when I was a kid. I'd slip out at night when I couldn't sleep anymore and roam the streets. On trash days, I'd always find neat stuff. I'd take anything apart to see how it worked, then see if I could fix it. I learned a lot about all sorts of gadgets. I'd read about them in the encyclopedia. People throw things away and buy new, but so many times there's a really easy fix."

"Figures," Sarah laughed. "So, you picked up a lawnmower and fixed it?"

"Just varnish buildup in the carburetor, which froze the needle valve so gas wasn't getting to the bowl. Very common after sitting awhile," Daniel said.

Sarah looked at him with a slight grimace, not understanding any of what he had said.

"The owner probably got tired of trying to start it and found it was cheaper to buy new than take it to the shop. I cleaned it, sharpened the blade, put in a new spark plug and gas, and it started right up. I could barely cut this grass with it, but that's because the grass is so thick. I take it no one has used this cage in a while."

"Impressive, Mr. Wizard," Sarah said, rolling her eyes in mock incredulousness. "I don't remember this cage ever being used, but it looks like you've been working pretty hard on it."

"The netting still has some holes, and I rigged a makeshift screen to throw from," Daniel said as he eased out under the netting to meet Sarah.

"Why? What's it for?"

"I'll be throwing from up close, not a regular pitching distance, so the screen will help me save my teeth from getting knocked out."

"Oh. I guess that makes good sense. Shows what I know, huh?"

"I also got an old home plate and some lime to teach Jonathan where to stand, and I hung a mat behind the plate with a target on it."

"So you try to hit the target, right?" Sarah asked as she looked over Daniel's handiwork.

"No, but it helps some. It's really to teach Jonathan how to watch the ball."

"Well, that I don't understand," Sarah said, "but I'll sit back and watch, and maybe learn, huh? Is that a bucket of tennis balls?"

"Yep," Daniel said as he held the netting up for Jonathan.

"Are we a little confused here? I thought this was baseball."

"Are you going to keep asking questions or can me and Jonathan get started?" Daniel said, sensing Jonathan's impatience.

"I'll shut up. I can take a hint," Sarah chuckled, retreating to the lawn chair she brought with her. "I've got cold beer in the cooler when you're done," she added after settling in. "It is Sunday, you know."

She noticed Daniel had turned his attention to Jonathan, so her quip had gone unheard. They took their positions in the cage and she watched as Daniel explained to Jonathan how to grip the bat, always telling him the *why* as well as the *what* and *how*. Then she noticed Jonathan had a new bat. Sarah watched as Daniel set his stance and patiently took Jonathan through the batting motions. The bat seemed to flow smoothly around Jonathan, like a natural extension, no longer clumsily.

Finally, Daniel picked up a baseball. *All right,* Sarah thought, *now for some real hitting!* But she frowned, her disappointment apparent, when Daniel instructed Jonathan to just stand there, ready, but not to swing.

"What part of 'do not swing' did you not understand, Jonathan?" Daniel chided light-heartedly after Jonathan swung at the pitch.

"I'm sorry, Mr. Daniel, I couldn't help it!" Jonathan said, hanging his head.

"Now this time, no swinging." Daniel, without raising his voice, added just enough emphasis to ensure Jonathan got the message.

"Okay," Jonathan said, clenching his teeth as he tried to concentrate on what Daniel wanted.

Daniel threw the ball and Sarah heard the *whup* as it hit the mat. Daniel paused, obviously perplexed. He walked toward Sarah.

"What's wrong, Daniel?" Sarah said.

"I'm just thinking," Daniel said pensively. "Trying to decide whether to curb Jonathan's fear of the ball first or teach him to watch it. I think I'll have to get rid of his fear first."

"What makes you think he's afraid of the ball?"

"Mom!" Jonathan called out impatiently, showing his annoyance.

"Chill out, Jonathan," Sarah retorted and turned her attention back to Daniel, coaxing an answer.

"Watch his left foot when I throw the ball," Daniel said. He walked back to the batting cage. "Get set, Jonathan, exactly like we went over."

Jonathan set himself, ready to bat, but Daniel came up and

readjusted, then explained. "Now, I'm going to do that a lot until you are so accustomed to your position that nothing else seems or feels right."

"What do you mean?" Jonathan asked, still not getting what Daniel was showing him.

"Yeah, explain." Sarah called out.

They had been there for thirty minutes, and a ball had not touched a bat yet. She popped open another beer and took a sip.

Daniel called to her. "Put the beer down for a second, Sarah, and cross your hands into a double fist, like this." Daniel intertwined his fingers. "You too, Jonathan." Jonathan dropped the bat and made a double fist. "Now, both of you tell me which thumb is on top. Right or left?" Both of them had their right thumb on top. "What? Are both of y'all weird or something?" Daniel said as he rolled his eyes. "Nobody puts their right thumb on top, unless they're from Texas or something!" They both looked at Daniel, not knowing exactly how to take this rebuke.

"I'm just kidding guys," Daniel grinned. "Lighten up. You and I both know there is no right or wrong way to cross your hands. But, try to do it now, putting your left thumb on top."

They both struggled for a second, having to think about the action before completing it.

"Doesn't it feel weird?" Daniel asked.

"Yes," they both uttered simultaneously.

"It's called muscle memory," Daniel explained. "You've crossed your hands thousands of times with your right thumb up, so to do the opposite takes a little thought and feels weird. The good thing is, there is no right or wrong here, so it doesn't matter. But when it comes to the mechanics of hitting a baseball, there are rights and wrongs. And Jonathan has already trained his muscles to do it wrong. Now, if you started crossing your hands with your left thumb up and practiced it ten thousand times, it would eventually feel normal and the other way would feel weird. So, I'm going to get Jonathan to stand, see, swing, and follow through correctly and practice it so many times that it, and only it, feels right. His muscles will have memorized that motion so when he gets to the plate, he will not think about the motion at all. His body will just do it. All he will think about is one thing, and only one thing."

"What?" Sarah asked impatiently.

"Seeing the ball," Daniel said. "It's the only thing he has time to think about and all that's important in the moment he has to hit the ball. He doesn't even have time to decide whether or not to hit the ball. He'll decide to hit the ball before it's pitched, then see it and either swing or check his swing if he decides not to hit."

"You're going to teach him all of that?" Sarah was doubtful.

"Of course. That's what we're here for."

"How can you be so confident?" Sarah asked.

"It's like figuring out if an egg is hardboiled or not," Daniel explained while Jonathan fidgeted and kept experimenting with clenching his fists different ways. "Easy if you know how, impossible if you don't. Look, let me tell you this and put some of your fears to rest. Nothing I'm going to teach Jonathan did I make up myself: I'm not even close to being that smart. Everything I will go over, and how I go over it, I was taught. And fortunately, I had very good teachers. Now, baseball has been around for a hundred and fifty years, and a lot of very smart people have figured out the best way to do everything there is to do in baseball. We don't have to invent anything here, especially at this level. We just need to learn it. Players get paid millions of dollars to swing a bat, and none of them invented a new way to swing. So, neither am I. What I am going to do is show Jonathan how the pros do it. I figure if it's good enough for a million-dollar player, then it's got to be good enough for us. And I will encourage you to watch the sports highlights on TV. Test out what I say. Watch closely for things I tell Jonathan. You'll see the game in a new light."

"Okay, okay! Sold! Can he hit a ball now?" Sarah asked hopefully.

"Nope, not even close yet."

"Crap. I think I'll go boil some eggs," Sarah said as she went back to the cooler.

Daniel turned so his back was to Sarah, picked up the bat and handed it to Jonathan. "Does your Mom drink beer much?"

"Not really," Jonathan said. "And not during the week. But on the weekends she gets sad sometimes and then drinks. But only light beer. She says it's not like real beer. But I know it is. I don't say anything, but I wish she wasn't sad."

"Hey you guys, quit jaw-jacking. I want to see some action out here!" Sarah was feeling feisty and enjoying watching Daniel with Jonathan. Jonathan seemed to be at ease with him, which was a miracle unto itself since he had never had a good relationship with a grown man.

Daniel reset Jonathan in the batter's box and stepped behind the pitching screen. "Okay, what are you not going to do?"

"Swing," said Jonathan, still not understanding why, but wanting to do what Daniel asked.

"Are you watching, Sarah?"

"Throw the ball, professor," Sarah replied, grinning.

Daniel threw the ball and watched Jonathan's reaction. "Did you see his left foot?" he said, looking toward Sarah. And then to Jonathan. "Why did you move your left foot back?"

"I don't know. I didn't know I did," Jonathan said. "Is that really bad?"

"It means you're afraid of the ball. Have you ever been hit by the ball?" Daniel asked.

"No," Jonathan shrugged.

"It only hurts if you get hit in the face. The helmet protects your head, and at your age the ball isn't going fast. Now, a ninety mile-per-hour fastball to the elbow hurts, but even so, you don't see the big-leaguers cry or shy away from the ball. And they get a free ride to first base. So, we need to get rid of your fear. When you step back with your left foot, where is your face?"

Jonathan shrugged again. Daniel was going fast. "Jonathan, that was a question. Let's get the answer. Now, get in the batter's box. Step back with your left foot. Where is your face pointed?"

"At you, I guess," he said.

"You guessed right. And where is the ball coming from?" Daniel pressed.

"You?"

"Right again. It's not rocket science, is it?"

"No, sir," Jonathan said, relieved.

"Let's cut the *sir* for a while and just say yes or no."

"But Mom told me to say it."

"Well, your mom is right, and even I say *sir* to anyone older or who I don't know, so it's a good habit. But while we're in the cage, let's drop it. I'll talk to your mom. We're going to be going fast, and I need you to talk to me, too. So let's just talk like friends while we're in here. Just you and me. Deal?"

"Yes, sir."

Daniel rolled his eyes.

Jonathan grinned. "I mean, yes."

"Much better. So, back to you wanting to stop the ball with your face. If the ball is coming from me and your face is toward me, what's going to happen?"

"I'm going to get hit in the face," Jonathan said, beginning to understand Daniel's logic.

"Gee, you're brilliant, kid, good deduction." Jonathan smiled as Daniel grinned.

"Now, here are two philosophies to avoid getting hit. First, make sure your side is toward the pitcher," Daniel demonstrated as he explained. "You're a lot thinner sideways than facing him, so there's less to hit. Also, all you have to do is rock forward or backward three or four inches, like this," Daniel leaned forward, then backward, "and the ball will go right by you. If you're lucky, it will graze you and you get on base with no pain. Now I don't suggest that method until later in your career, so here's what we're going to learn."

Daniel showed Jonathan how to turn away from the ball if he couldn't avoid getting hit. "It either glances off your back, hits your butt or helmet, or the back of your leg. All well-padded, so not much pain and no damage, like teeth getting knocked out. But remember, you've never been hit and probably won't get hit, so we need to get you to stop worrying about it."

Daniel took the bucket of tennis balls and went to the pitcher's position. "All right, get in position and do not swing. And most important, don't move your foot. If you move your foot, I'll hit you with the next pitch. Fair deal?"

"No!" Jonathan said, fearfully.

"Well, it's the only deal you've got. Ready?"

"No." Jonathan pleaded.

"Yes, you are." Daniel threw a tennis ball as an inside pitch, close to Jonathan. Jonathan stepped back and before he could regain position, Daniel hit him in the chest with another ball. Sarah was on her feet by now, watching intently, restraining herself from interfering.

"Hey, that's not fair. I wasn't ready!" Jonathan protested.

"Did it hurt?"

"No." Jonathan admitted.

"Of course it didn't. It's a stupid tennis ball. But you still moved your foot. Get set again. No. Your back foot is wrong and your wrist is cocked." Jonathan adjusted. "Much better." Daniel threw a ball, and Jonathan stayed planted in position.

"See? I knew you could do it. Again." Daniel continued until there were no more tennis balls. Daniel picked up another ball and threw it. Jonathan heard the *whup* of the ball hitting the mat before he realized it was a baseball. "Look at your feet, Jonathan," Daniel said quickly. Jonathan had held his position as the baseball flew by. Daniel picked up the remaining baseballs and pitched them; the boy did not flinch or step away.

Sarah just stared at her son, like watching a boy become a man; she had just witnessed him conquer a fear. For Jonathan, it wasn't a big deal; he was ready to continue. For Daniel, it was just another lesson taught. But for Sarah it was an epiphany, a moment in life she knew would stay with her forever. She couldn't explain it and would never share it, but as only a mother can know, she knew her son was a new person. Her little boy was gone.

Daniel broke her reverie with his next question. "Okay, Jonathan, where did the ball hit the mat?" Jonathan looked at the mat quizzically, then back at Daniel, then at the mat again. He pointed to a place on the mat, not having any idea where the ball hit, but not wanting to disappoint; he just vaguely pointed.

"Not even close, Jonathan. Why don't you know where it hit the mat?"

"Because I didn't see it!" Jonathan said defensively.

"Exactly! Best answer you could have given and the only honest one. Always best to be honest, Jonathan. For two reasons. The first is you're not smart enough to remember all the lies." Sarah reddened with sudden anger, ready to defend her son's intelligence. "But don't worry, Jonathan, nobody is smart enough to remember lies."

"And what's the other one?" Sarah piped in, relieved by Daniel's finesse with the intellect reasoning.

"I don't ask questions I don't already know the answer to."

"So why ask the question?"

"To hear someone else's answer, for one. To learn how someone lies, for another. But probably just to get the answer out in the open," Daniel said.

"So, you don't ask questions just to learn the answer?"

"What you learn is what the other person wants to tell you, which may or may not have anything to do with the truth or the answer."

"We have quite a cynical side, don't we, Mr. Furman?" Sarah asked with a facetious air, lightening the didactic conversation.

"Mom, can you let us practice now? Please?" Jonathan's annoyance with his mom's interruption was clear since he was beginning to understand Daniel's instructions.

"Okay, Coach, back to work. I'll go sip my beer. How much longer, by the way?"

"We're almost done."

"See, Mom," Jonathan blurted, "you just wasted all my time."

"Cool it, Jonathan. I'm sure Daniel isn't going to quit early on you. Are you, Daniel?" She turned and headed back to her chair. Daniel noticed her walk. *Nice, smooth stride,* he thought as he took a deep breath, *and more.*

"Okay, Jonathan, uh, where were we? Umm. Oh, yeah. Why didn't you see where the ball hit the mat? You didn't see it because you weren't watching the ball." Daniel strode back to the pitcher's station and picked up a baseball. "Get set, Jonathan."

"Can I swing now?" Jonathan asked, hopefully.

"Nope."

"When?" Jonathan didn't hide his disappointment.

"When you can see the ball all the way to the catcher's mitt."

"I can do that!" Jonathan was adamant.

Daniel threw the ball, and Jonathan's head did not move. "So where did the ball hit the mat?"

"I don't know; I forgot to look."

"So you can't see the ball to the catcher's mitt yet, can you?"

"No," Jonathan said dejectedly.

"Well, let's learn," Daniel said reassuringly. "I want you to get set and decide to hit the ball. Then follow the ball from my hand to the mat. No swinging. Just tell me exactly where the ball hits. Ready?"

"Yep." Jonathan's dejection faded as he concentrated on this new task.

Whup. Jonathan heard the ball hit but missed the moment of impact.

"Again, Jonathan. This time move your head with the ball. Concentrate on my hand, then the ball, and follow it." Daniel was showing him as he talked.

Whup. Jonathan saw the point of contact and pointed it out. He saw the ball in Daniel's hand; he saw the ball fly by him and he followed it to the mat. Again and again Daniel threw the ball and Jonathan followed it. Each time he got set exactly the same way and watched the ball to the mat. "Great job, Jonathan," Daniel said. "Great job!"

"So can I swing now?" Jonathan's excitement with his success was evident.

"Tomorrow, Jonathan. You can swing tomorrow."

"Aw, come on, just one swing." Jonathan pleaded.

"You need to learn to trust me. Wait 'til tomorrow."

"But I want to hit today. I can see the ball!" Jonathan argued.

"Then get set." Daniel threw the strike, and Jonathan heard the *whup* of the mat before the bat moved.

"That's not fair!" Jonathan protested.

"Life's not fair sometimes, Jonathan; but tomorrow you can swing, I promise. Let's pick up the balls. I think your mom's snoozing. Look." They looked over and saw the beer can sideways at Sarah's feet and her chin on her chest. *She looks peaceful,* Daniel thought. *It must be nice to be able to fall asleep anywhere like that.*

"Let's pack the car, then wake her up," Daniel said. "I'll come back later for the lawn mower and my car."

"Thanks, Mr. Daniel. Thanks a lot."

"You're welcome. We'll hit the ball tomorrow. I know today was work, but tomorrow will be fun." Daniel promised.

"I had fun today," Jonathan said, smiling at Daniel.

"When's your next game?"

"Thursday."

"Well, that gives us three more practices before your game."

"So, you're going to come out here every evening with me?" Jonathan gushed.

"That's the plan. We have a lot of work to do to get you up to par."

"Am I that bad, Daniel?" Jonathan grimaced.

"No! Absolutely not. But learning the right way to hit a baseball is not easy. It takes a lot of work. You know there are a thousand ways to do it wrong, so we have to make sure none of those ways creep into your swing. That takes practice and more practice. But you're a good learner and good listener, so you'll do great."

"Thanks, Mr. Daniel. I can wait 'til tomorrow."

CHAPTER 10

the art of the spin

"Jonathan, grab that bucket please, and let's head over to the bench." Daniel motioned to the bucket of balls, paddles and rolls, and the charts he had stuffed into his small car.

"Not the cage?" Jonathan was disappointed. He had really enjoyed the last two afternoons of hitting.

"No. Maybe later if we have time, but today is a classroom session. We're going to learn about ball movement."

Jonathan sighed and picked up the bucket. There were empty toilet paper rolls on top.

"What are these for?" Jonathan quizzed.

"You'll see. Just bring those, too," Daniel said.

"Ping-pong balls, tennis balls, soccer ball, paddles, an old racquet. I don't see any baseballs in here," Jonathan said.

"There's one in there somewhere. Just come on. We've got a lot to learn this afternoon, and I need to leave early to get to Galveston."

"Okay." Jonathan struggled with his part of the loot and dropped it by the picnic table.

"Catch this," Daniel said as he picked up one of the empty toilet paper rolls and flicked it at Jonathan, spinning it between his hands as he released it. It curved sharply to the left as Jonathan grabbed for it.

"Try again." Daniel picked up another roll and flicked it, spinning it the opposite direction. As Jonathan reached for it, it curved sharply to the right, and he missed it.

"One more time, Jonathan." Daniel picked up a roll and flicked it, this time putting topspin on it. The roll hit the ground at Jonathan's feet before he could grab it. Jonathan looked at Daniel with a *What gives?* look, and Daniel knew his demonstration was nearing Jonathan's frustration point. "Okay, this time you will be able to catch it, but it will loop before it gets to you. Ready?" Daniel backed up two steps and flicked the roll with backspin. It did a tight loop and floated into Jonathan's hands.

"Now, what was the difference in those throws, Jonathan?"

"The spin. You spun them differently," Jonathan said.

"Exactly," Daniel explained. "Balls act the same way when they spin, and we're going to learn about that today, and why."

Jonathan shrugged, obviously disappointed he wasn't hitting.

"Look, Jonathan," Daniel said, wanting to get him to understand the importance of the lesson, but knowing that without Jonathan's support it would be time wasted. "The last two days you've gotten to where you are hitting the ball great. Your stance, your look, your swing. It's all becoming innate."

"*In eight?* What's *in eight* mean?" Jonathan asked, not hiding his displeasure about not hitting.

"*Innate.* I-N-N-A-T-E. One word. It means you feel it with your soul. It's a part of you now so you don't have to think about it. Your body moves without you having to concentrate on it. It's just natural. It didn't start out that way at all, but we learned, developed, and practiced until now it's innate. But I was throwing the balls very straight and with very little spin, so all you had to do was swing the same way at the same ball every time. The batter's box isn't like that. I wanted you to hit the ball; the pitcher wants you to miss. And he's going to do everything he can to fool you and make you miss it. And he will do that by changing the speed and spin. What you have to do is learn how the ball moves and why, so when the ball leaves the pitcher's hand, you will *innately* know how it is moving, and your body will react without you thinking about it. Get it?"

A car door slammed and Daniel saw Sarah walking toward them. She had obviously come straight from work, since she was very early. Daniel watched her for a moment as she was looking down at the stepping stones, making sure her high heels did not miss the hard surfaces. Daniel had not seen her while at work since the first day, only talked with her on the phone, and when he saw her at the field, she was usually in sweats or jeans and a sweat shirt. Today she looked stunning. *What is it about high heels that is so mesmerizing?* he thought.

"I get it," Jonathan said without getting Daniel's attention. "I said *I get it*, Daniel. What now?" The urgency in Jonathan's voice was building as he willed Daniel back from his daydreaming.

"Oh, yeah, good. Uh, well now." Daniel was having trouble regaining his train of presentation as Sarah got to the table.

"Yes, professor, what now?" she chided.

Daniel shrugged off his embarrassment and launched into an explanation of spinning balls.

"So, no batting today? Jonathan has barely done anything for the past two days except talk about hitting the ball. And at breakfast, he said he couldn't wait for school to be over so he could get to the cage. I left work early just to see him for myself. So, what now?"

"Sorry, Sarah," Daniel replied. "Jonathan has been doing great in the cage, but I need to push things along before his game tomorrow night. I was just about to introduce the Bernoulli Principle to him."

"The *Bear-what* principle?"

"It's how planes fly and how balls move when they spin," Daniel started to explain.

"Daniel! How planes fly? Really? Isn't that a bit advanced for Jonathan?"

"Well, Dad used to get a lot of flak from parents when he taught this at such an early age, but he told me that although very few of the players would get it, it planted the seed. He said some of the players would get it, and it may spark an intellect that will lead to further education. And some of the players would never get it but would just learn by experience. Either way, it was beneficial. He equated it to learning to read: you never knew exactly when you learned to read, but one day you were just reading. But the teachers knew they built the knowledge into you, step by step. This is a pretty big step, for sure, and you never know exactly where it will lead, if anywhere."

"Okay, Plato, I won't interrupt again. But I wouldn't mind seeing a hit or two since I took off work for it."

"I'll see what I can do for you," Daniel conceded.

"Now, can we finish, Mom, so I can get into the cage?" Jonathan grumbled.

Daniel started presenting the principles of air movement and pressure to Jonathan, using props and diagrams his father had made and used many times. He used ping-pong balls and tennis balls to show Jonathan how certain spins and movement created high and low pressure on the surface of the ball, *pushing* it off a natural path. He let Jonathan experiment with the different balls, each one marked so the spin could be seen. Then he showed Jonathan the baseball, and how the seams on the baseball are raised and made with red thread, which makes them visible if you know to look for them. He explained how the raised seams affect the air movement around the ball, like paddles through water, pointing out that most other balls like tennis balls, ping-pong balls, and soccer balls did not have this feature. Then Daniel showed Jonathan how to hold the baseball so either two or four of the seams acted like paddles.

"So that's what they're talking about when they say two-seam fastball?" Jonathan asked.

"Exactly!" Daniel applauded that his student was understanding. "And a four-seam fastball is going to move slightly more than a two-seam fastball. Now, the neat thing about baseball is all the spin has to be generated by the pitcher's hand, so you really have to watch each part of his windup and how he releases it to see how he's spinning it. If you do, then you'll know how it's going to move. Does that make sense?"

"Yes, sir! I mean, yes."

"With tennis racquets, it's easy to figure out how the ball is going to spin because you can see how your opponent holds the racquet and hits the ball." Daniel picked up an old wooden tennis racquet and a few old balls and went through the motions with Jonathan, each time quizzing him on which way the ball was going to curve, or rise, or drop quickly. Jonathan was as quick a study as Daniel had ever seen from any of the players his father had taught. And Daniel praised the youngster as he progressed. Finally, Daniel looked at his watch and said, "We have a few minutes left. Let's hit the cage."

Jonathan grabbed his bat and ran to the cage while Daniel got his glove and a bucket of baseballs and headed that way, Sarah pulling up the rear while trying not to bury her heels in the ground. Finally, she took them off and caught up with Daniel.

"You really think he understood all that, Daniel?" she asked so Jonathan couldn't hear.

"He understood enough of it, and more than most kids his age. He's very bright, you know."

"Of course, I think so, I'm his mother. But I worry he's not learning nearly enough. His grades are okay, but it's very hard to hold his interest in a subject."

"I think his mother is being too hard on herself," Daniel said. "He told me what you did when you found out the public school no longer taught cursive writing. You taught it to him."

"I was livid!" Sarah snorted. "What the hell has gotten into our school systems these days? I probably should send him to a private school."

"He doesn't need a private school, Sarah. He has you. An involved parent is the most important part of a kid's education, and from what he tells me, you're the best."

Sarah looked up at Daniel, for the first time seeing his height and his serenely blue eyes. "Thank you, Daniel," she said quietly. "You don't know how much it means to me to hear that."

"Well, it's true. Gotta go. I have an impatient student over there."

Sarah laughed and watched him pull up the netting and ease into the cage.

"All right, Jonathan, here's what we're going to do. You are not going to swing," Daniel announced. Jonathan hit the plate with his bat, suddenly furious with disappointment.

"JONATHAN!" Sarah immediately barked. But Daniel held up his hand, and Sarah eased off her rebuke.

"Before you get upset, Jonathan," Daniel continued, "let me finish."

"Yes, sir," Jonathan said, responding to his mother's stare.

"I'm going to throw the first ball, and you're going to watch the way it spins and tell me how it moves and where it hits the mat. If you get it right, then you can swing at the next ball. Fair enough?"

"Yes, sir!" Jonathan's excitement was back.

"Look for the seams, Jonathan."

Daniel threw the ball, spinning it counter-clockwise. Jonathan concentrated and followed the ball to the mat, indicating with the tip of his bat where it hit and then turning his finger counter-clockwise, telling Daniel the ball moved away from him. Sarah was speechless.

"Perfect!" Daniel said. "Now, swing away. Don't get careless. Get your left foot in position." Jonathan looked down and rotated his foot slightly. Sarah was again impressed. Daniel threw a ball, and Sarah watched as her son's body weight shifted into the pitch, hips fluidly rotating as the bat glided around and met the ball perfectly, sending it straight back toward Daniel's face. She gasped as it hit the frame of the screen and fell to the ground. Sarah felt the chills course over her body, pride in her son welling up.

"Fantastic!" she heard Daniel say. "Now time to watch." Jonathan continued indicating spin and movements and being rewarded with a swing until the bucket was empty. Daniel came from behind the screen and gave Jonathan a high five.

"Listen, Jonathan. I'm going to ask you to do something you won't like, but it's very important."

"What?" Jonathan was leery.

"You'll be playing the Reds tomorrow, right?"

"Yes, sir."

"And Douglas is pitching?"

"That's what I heard at school."

"All right," Daniel said. "Now, getting in the batter's box is a whole lot different than the cage with me throwing to you. Doubts creep in, nerves act up, old habits come roaring back like a freight train, and all this work vaporizes like a summer fog."

"I promise that won't happen," Jonathan stammered.

"That's not a promise you can keep, Jonathan. Believe me. But listen carefully and do what I say and we can overcome it, and you won't have to promise anything except to do one thing for me."

"Okay, Daniel, I promise."

"Douglas throws a lot of junk," Daniel said. "I watched him last Saturday. And he doesn't throw many strikes, but he throws high, and at your age, a high ball looks heaven sent and every kid loves to swing at them. Except you. I don't want you to swing at anything. Promise?"

"Promise, Daniel." Jonathan was dejected.

"I'm going to try to make it to your game, but if I don't, I want you to signal to your mom after every pitch which way the ball was spinning. Use your fingers like this, very quickly, so nobody knows what you're doing except us. Also, make sure you act like you're going to swing and check your swing. If you don't, the umpire will think you're just watching the ball, hoping for a walk, and he'll call a ball a strike just to make you swing. But if you check your swing, he'll think you were just smart enough to see it wasn't a good ball to hit and he'll call it honestly. Got it?"

"Yes, sir," Jonathan said quietly.

"Now, with Douglas, if you never swing, you'll have an eighty percent chance of walking, which means you will be on base for the first time and you'll get to learn how it feels. So, when you do get your first hit, you'll be prepared for base running. Do you understand all of this?"

"Yes, sir. I got it. And I'll do it. Are you going to be there?" Jonathan asked, hopefully.

"I'll do my best, but I can't absolutely promise."

"I hope you can make it," Jonathan said, enthusiastically.

"Me too. Look, I'm late for Galveston. Can you and your mom clean up here and I'll pick the stuff up from you after the game?"

"We'll take care of it, Daniel," he heard Sarah's voice chime in. "You go on."

"Thanks."

"No. Thank you. That was incredible," Sarah said.

"Jonathan's a pretty incredible kid. That makes my job very easy," Daniel said as he playfully pulled the brim of Jonathan's hat over his eyes.

"Like standing an egg on its end?" Sarah quipped.

"Yeah, like standing an egg on its end." Daniel laughed and ran toward his car. Halfway there he spun once, waved, and continued without missing a stride.

Showoff, Sarah thought, smiling, and started picking up the props from Daniel's outdoor classroom while Jonathan gathered the balls inside the net. She heard the throaty exhaust of his sports car and a little chirp from his rear tires as he hit second gear going out of the parking lot.

"Does he drive like that with you, Jonathan?"

"No, ma'am. He's very careful with me in the car," Jonathan said.

"Good. Do you know what kind of car it is? It looks old."

"It's like ancient," Jonathan said, not looking up from gathering the balls. "It's from the sixties he told me. It's a Porsche, but I forgot what number. Nine something, I think."

"Ancient, huh? And what does that make me?"

"Aw, Mom, you're not ancient. You're beautiful," he said, finally looking up at his mom.

"Jonathan, what a sweet thing to say."

"Everybody says so, Mom."

"Everybody?" Sarah said as she knitted her brow, showing concern.

"Well, a lot of people. You know, all my friends, and all the coaches," Jonathan confessed.

"The coaches talk about me?"

"Not really. I just heard them say you're the best-looking mom out here."

"Well, that's heartwarming," Sarah said, doubting Jonathan could detect the sarcasm in her voice.

"Well, Daniel likes you!" Jonathan said defensively.

"Did Daniel say that to you?"

"No, ma'am . . . but he looks at you."

"What do you mean *he looks at me*?"

"He watches you walk and forgets we're practicing!"

"When did you see this?"

"One time last week when you were walking away, and tonight when you were coming to the table over there. I know he likes you, Mom. He's happy when you're around, and laughs."

"He's not happy when y'all are alone?" Sarah asked.

"It's not that! He's just more," Jonathan searched for the word, "he's just more serious, that's all."

"Well, that makes sense, Jonathan, but it doesn't mean any more than we're friends."

"But couldn't you go out on a date with him?" Jonathan asked.

"No, Jonathan."

"Why?"

"There are many reasons, the first of which, he hasn't asked me, and I doubt if he ever would."

"You don't know that, Mom."

"I'm pretty sure about it. Besides, we're both executives at VCM, so us dating would be very frowned upon."

"How come?" Jonathan said, not hiding his frustration with adult issues.

"I write his progress reports and evaluations for Victor, so I have to remain objective, and he has to trust I'm fair with all the associates, as do they."

She saw the disappointment on Jonathan's face, and for the first time it occurred to her that it may not have been wise to ask Daniel for help. She feared her acquaintance with Daniel would probably be short-lived as he established his own set of friends, in his own age group, in Houston. She knew when that happened, Jonathan would watch another man disappear from his life. Daniel was the first man he responded positively to for as long as she could remember. She made the mental note to be more careful in the future and keep men at bay for a while.

"Daniel's a very nice young man, Jonathan," Sarah said, "and if I was ten years younger, I would definitely be interested in him. But he's just a friend helping you, so let's leave it at that."

"Well, your age shouldn't matter!" Jonathan said with finality.

Sarah smiled weakly. She wished her son had a good father figure in his life but was doubtful that would happen. She felt that the men with whom she connected were turned on by her beauty but turned off by her intelligence, and that left her with a gnawing distrust of relationships. But Daniel seemed not to be overawed by her looks, nor intimidated by her intelligence. And she wondered what a relationship with him would be like.

CHAPTER 11

playing baseball

"**D**aniel! Glad you could make it! Jonathan was so worried you wouldn't be here." Sarah was in the bleachers, on a lower row than usual, hoping Jonathan would remember Daniel's instructions.

"Is Douglas pitching?" Daniel asked as he eased his way up the bleachers to Sarah.

"Yes. And it's just like you predicted. I've been counting balls and strikes." Sarah showed Daniel the pad with her tally. "If those boys would quit swinging at high pitches, they would all walk."

"That's always one of the hardest things to teach young players. But at their height and with the ball speed, a high pitch looks perfect coming in. Then they have to 'tomahawk' to hit it."

"Your percentage of balls and strikes is amazingly accurate, too. How did you get that so fast?" Sarah looked at Daniel with her eyebrow raised. He loved that look.

"It wasn't hard," he settled in beside her.

"I know, I know. Like figuring out if an egg is boiled," Sarah conceded.

"Yeah. When does Jonathan bat?" Daniel saw him running in from right field.

"He just went in this inning, and they're coming off the field, so I think he's the second batter if they put him in the same batting position as the right fielder was."

"Good! I'm glad I made it in time." Daniel watched Jonathan come out onto the on-deck circle and focus his attention on the pitcher. He took a couple of practice swings and then set his stance. His head moved perfectly with the ball, and as it hit the catcher's mitt, he turned and motioned to his mom. He saw Daniel and smiled. Daniel indicated he had seen the pitch correctly and smiled back.

"He's a really good kid, Sarah. You should be very proud," Daniel said, keeping his eyes on Jonathan.

"Right now, I'm very nervous. My stomach is doing flips. I think I liked it better when I knew he was going to strike out. Just kidding, of course, but he is so excited about getting up to the plate now. I just hope he isn't let down."

"He'll be fine, Sarah. Don't worry. He has a lot of baseball left in him. One time at bat isn't going to make or break him."

"I wish I had your confidence," she groaned.

"Well, Jonathan's just seen four pitches accurately, three balls and one strike, but the batter swung at two balls and is out. Too bad."

At the third swing and miss, Daniel heard a father who was sitting in front of Sarah make a loud, derogatory remark about the batter. Daniel's senses were suddenly on edge. He watched as Jonathan stepped into the batter's box. He held his hand up to the umpire until he was set perfectly and then gripped the bat as Daniel taught, and put his eyes on the pitcher's glove where the boy held the ball, waiting for Jonathan to get set. Daniel stood quietly and motioned to Sarah to trade places with him. Sarah shrugged and moved. The pitch came in high and outside, a curve ball, and Jonathan stepped back, adjusted his helmet with two fingers, indicating the pitch, and stepped back in and reset himself. The second pitch was a fast ball inside, and Sarah let out a gasp as she saw Jonathan lean backwards slightly as the pitch flew inches from his chest. She grabbed Daniel's knee, her mother's instinct screaming for her son's safety. Jonathan acted as if nothing untoward had happened. The boy put one finger on the back of his helmet and angled it to the left.

"Inside fast ball. Perfect," Daniel whispered to Sarah. Sarah was so nervous she could hardly breathe. The third pitch was a perfect strike, a fast ball down the middle. Jonathan moved his hips into it, started to take the swing and checked at the last moment.

The parent, now in front of Daniel, stood up and yelled at Jonathan, "What are you waiting for, kid? That was a perfect pitch! Are you blind?"

Immediately, Daniel's face was in the man's ear. "One more remark like that and I'm going to shove a bat up your ass so far you can pick your teeth with it! Now sit down and shut up!" The parent jumped around with fists clenched. Daniel calmly turned his hat around backward and stared down at the man, his six-foot-two-inch frame towering above the parent. The parent glared at Sarah. Daniel calmly asked, "Well, are you going to sit down?" The parent, trying to save face, hesitated, then sat slowly.

"Good move," Daniel said quietly and sat down behind him, leaning forward on the bleacher bench so the man could feel his presence. Sarah exhaled, not realizing she had been holding her breath. Jonathan smiled at his mom and stepped back into the batter's box. The next pitch was an outside curve ball that could have been called either way. The umpire indicated a strike as Jonathan signaled the pitch.

"That was a great pitch not to hit," Daniel said to Sarah. "It's almost impossible to get a good swing at it, and if you do, it's going to the first or second baseman with nothing on it. And that's an easy out." Sarah noticed her tally pad was a crumpled heap in her hand. The pitcher, flush with the success tried the pitch again, but this time he missed the outside corner, and the umpire nonchalantly motioned a ball. Now the count was full, and even Daniel could feel his heart beating faster but remained outwardly calm. The pitcher then went for another fast ball down the middle, and Jonathan again started his motion and checked as the ball flew by his face. "High, ball four," the umpire said and indicated to Jonathan to take his base. Jonathan turned and tossed his bat toward the dugout, quickly gave a thumbs up to his mom, and trotted to first base.

"Jonathan's going to steal second on the first pitch," Daniel said. "Pray the batter doesn't pop it up."

"How do you know that?" Sarah quickly asked. The parent in front of Daniel turned as if to ask the same question. He continued listening.

"I told him to."

"You WHAT? What if he gets thrown out?" Sarah exclaimed.

"If he doesn't hesitate, he will make it with half a second to spare, even if the throw is perfect," Daniel explained.

"How can you be so sure?"

"Timing," Daniel said. "Watch the catcher, but first watch the pitch. Ninety percent of the time this pitcher starts with a curve ball, which is much slower than his fast ball. That gives Jonathan an extra tenth of a second. Then the catcher will double pump the ball, which means he catches it, takes it out, touches his glove again, and then throws it. A very bad habit for a catcher. You'll see infielders do it when they have plenty of time for the throw to first. It looks cool, so young players pick up the habit. But it costs the catcher almost a whole second. The difference between a successful steal and not is just a fraction of a second. Jonathan can steal in four and a half seconds, and the catcher, without double pumping and with a fast ball, can get the ball to second in four seconds. So, if Jonathan takes off the instant the pitcher has committed his throw, and he throws a curve ball, and the catcher double pumps, then Jonathan will beat the throw to second by at least a half a second, which is forever in baseball. Now, all bets are off if the batter pops up, because then Jonathan has to haul it back to first before the ball is caught and thrown to first for the double play."

Sarah just looked at Daniel, shaking her head. The baseball math was making her dizzy. Daniel hadn't taken his focus off the game during the entire explanation.

The pitcher threw the ball, and Jonathan was halfway to second by the time the batter fouled the ball away. Jonathan went back to first, where his coach was waiting, furious, because Jonathan had not been given the steal sign. Jonathan looked up at Daniel and grinned.

"Why's he grinning?" Sarah asked.

"I told him that might happen, but not to let it bother him, just look at me. I just gave him the steal sign again. He was halfway to second and would have made it standing up if he had wanted. He got a great jump, and the pitcher threw one of the slowest curves he's thrown yet, so Jonathan had it made. The pitcher will probably throw a fast ball this time, so Jonathan will have to really be quick off the base and have a good lead off. *Ooooh*." Daniel said, "The pitcher is going to try a pickoff."

At that moment, the pitcher rotated and threw to first. Jonathan dove back to the base as the first baseman caught the ball and put his glove on Jonathan, too late.

"God, I'm going to have a heart attack!" Sarah said, "Where did he learn that move?"

"You shouldn't sleep so much at the cage," Daniel teased. "You miss the finer points of your son's training."

"You're such an ass," Sarah said, elbowing Daniel. "Is he going to try to steal again?"

"Yep," Daniel said. "He'll make it easy this time. See how the pitcher is positioning his hand in the glove? He's gonna throw another curve."

The pitcher, throwing from the stretch position, moved his left leg up toward home plate, and at that instant Jonathan took off. The pitch was outside and the catcher caught, double pumped, and threw. It was a good throw, and the shortstop ran over to field the ball, but Jonathan slid into second well ahead of the throw. The first base coach took his hat off and threw it down in disgust. But the steal was successful, so he couldn't be but so angry with Jonathan.

"You're going to have to talk to the coach after the game, Daniel," Sarah chided.

"Yep. I think you're right," Daniel admitted. "But look at Jonathan; he's watching his third base coach now, just like we talked about."

"Why is the center fielder moving in?"

"They're going to try to pick Jonathan off at second using the center fielder. Two things have to get to second base to pick him off—a player and the ball. So, he just has to beat the player back if they try a pickoff."

"Damn, this is nerve-wracking," Sarah said, and Daniel noticed her legs were twitching restlessly.

"The pitcher is going to throw to the batter this time," Daniel said.

"How do you know?" Sarah asked, trying to see what Daniel was watching.

"The catcher just took a sign from his coach and shook his head. Pick-off move is off," Daniel explained.

"Oh. Does Jonathan know?" Sarah asked as she looked from the coach to the catcher, but saw nothing.

"I think so, but I'm not positive. But he did just take an extra step in his lead off the bag."

The pitcher threw the ball, a high strike the batter swung at and missed. The catcher caught the ball, double-pumped and threw to second, but again was late as Jonathan was already back on the base. Jonathan glanced up at Daniel and then watched his third base coach giving the bunt sign to the batter. A successful bunt would allow Jonathan to get to third base and be in scoring position.

Jonathan again took a large lead off the bag and quickly glanced around to make sure the center fielder and second baseman were holding their positions. The pitcher glanced back at Jonathan and then turned to deliver the pitch. The batter squared around for the bunt, and Jonathan started for third base. Sarah jumped off the bleacher seat to watch as the ball dribbled off the bat. By the time the catcher picked up the ball, Jonathan was sliding into third, so he turned his attention to first base and threw the batter out.

Jonathan was up immediately and taking steps toward home as he was watching the play unfold. The catcher had drifted too far away from home plate when fielding the ball and left it unguarded. Jonathan ran, his coach screaming for him to return to third. By the time the first baseman caught the ball and threw it back to the catcher Jonathan slid in safely and scored his first run without swinging a bat. He jumped up and bounced his way back to the dugout as Sarah was pounding on Daniel's arm, screaming at him through the roar of the crowd.

"Did you teach him that, Daniel? Well, did you? DID you?"

Daniel laughed so hard at Sarah's antics he couldn't answer. As they sat again, she demanded an answer.

"No, Sarah, I did not. You can't teach that. It's instinct. Jonathan reacted to the situation. I just gave him the tools he needed to know how to see the game. But that was all Jonathan."

"I don't believe you. Not for one instant!" she said.

"It's true. Your son's a baseball player. But I'll have a talk with his coaches, and I promise not to coach him from the stands again. It's not fair to his coaches."

As the game ended, the man in front of Daniel turned to him. "I'm sorry for mouthing off."

Daniel nodded to him and shook his hand. "Kids need encouraging, not berating. Yell for them, not at them and we'll all have fun."

CHAPTER 12

jonathan's first hit

"Are you ready to get a hit today?" Daniel asked Jonathan as they got out of the car and headed toward the baseball fields. Jonathan slung his bag over his back as Sarah gathered the water and snacks and followed, watching Daniel and Jonathan interact like they had known each other all their lives.

"Yes, sir, Daniel. I mean, yes." Daniel slapped the brim of Jonathan's hat playfully, knowing Jonathan was making the mistake on purpose—his way of poking fun at Daniel.

"And what's the most important thing to remember when you're in the box?"

"Watch the ball," Jonathan replied.

"Great!" Daniel said. "And when are you going to decide to hit the ball?"

"Before the pitcher throws it."

"Dang, you're smart, kid. Did your mom teach you all that?"

"She sure did. She's the best and prettiest baseball mom out here!" Jonathan said, trying to trip Daniel as they walked. Daniel sidestepped quickly and Jonathan's foot just caught air.

"Right again, kid. Have fun out there. That's really the most important thing, right?"

"Yep," Jonathan said as he split off to join his teammates.

"You think he'll do okay?" Sarah asked.

"He'll be fine, Sarah. Relax and enjoy the game," Daniel said.

"Easy for you to say, Mr. Baseball. But I'm his mom, and I worry. You know we're playing Eric's team again, don't you?"

"Yes," Daniel said.

"Do you know who'll be pitching?" Sarah asked.

"My guess is Benjamin. They need this win to lock in the season championship, so I'd say Eric will throw his best at us and go for another slaughter."

"Did you talk with Jonathan's coaches like you promised?"

"I did, *Mom*," Daniel wise cracked.

"Oh, shut up. You know I'm just fretful."

"I know. Sorry," Daniel said as they made their way up the bleachers.

"So, what did you say to them?" Sarah continued.

"I thought you were dropping this conversation?" Daniel smirked.

"Can't you just talk to me a little? I mean, he is my son, and they are his team, and I really would like to know what's going on," Sarah said.

Daniel smiled and relented. "Actually, I rearranged their lineup and changed some of their players' positions in the field."

"You did WHAT? You were supposed to apologize and tell them you'd stay out of their business!" Sarah yelled.

"I did apologize," Daniel said. "Then we got to talking and I starting asking them about their players, and their speed, and just general stuff. And they started asking questions, then asking for advice, and I started giving it, and before long I had rearranged their whole team. It's a much stronger lineup and a better defense. I also showed them where to move their players to better defensive positions on the field, and not moving them just because they think a kid may hit to a certain place. They really don't know what to do, Sarah. Everything they've learned, they learned when they were kids playing baseball. And most of it is wrong."

"Well, I hope they took it well. You know how coaches think they know everything and hate to be told they don't," Sarah lamented.

"I think they saw that what I said made sense, so they listened." Daniel said. "If they don't want the advice, that's okay. There's no money riding on the game. It's just kids having fun."

"I know, Daniel. I didn't mean to sound harsh. Thanks for talking to them."

"You're welcome," Daniel said. "Can we sit down now and get something to drink?"

"Sure," Sarah said, "But first, tell me where Jonathan is batting."

"Ninth."

"Ninth? I thought he could hit the ball now. Why didn't you move him up in the order?"

Daniel smiled. All parents want their kid to bat number one and play shortstop. It's a coach's nightmare. Daniel patiently explained the strategy. "Well, he hasn't hit the ball in a game, yet. And, the other team doesn't know he can hit the ball, so they won't take him seriously. Being underestimated by an opponent is a great weapon to have in your arsenal. And, when he does hit, the top of the lineup is behind him and capable of bringing him home."

"Oh," Sarah said, still not satisfied. "So, who's hitting first?"

Daniel glanced sideways at her realizing she was going to needle him for every drop of information she could. "Robby."

"Robby?" she exclaimed. "He's always batted seventh. He doesn't get many hits and he's too small to hit it very far. Why is he first?"

"He's the fastest runner and his size gives him a small strike zone, so he walks more than anyone on the team," Daniel explained patiently as he watched the teams warm up.

"Oh," Sarah said.

Daniel knew another question was coming.

"So why does he hit first just because he runs faster than anyone else?"

"You're not giving up, are you?" Daniel laughed.

"Well, getting information from you is like pulling a camel through the eye of a needle. Can't you just tell me what you told his coaches?"

"You want me to condense a three-hour meeting about baseball strategy and player assessment into five minutes?" Daniel said, knowing the answer but still asking just to aggravate Sarah. He was enjoying her playful but snarky attitude. He was happy she was comfortable enough with him to pester him unmercifully.

"You met for three hours?" she said. "I thought you were going to see them for five minutes just to apologize. Why didn't you tell me?"

"I didn't know you wanted to know," he said.

"Men are nuts. Of course I want to know! Why would I not want to know?" she hammered.

Daniel laughed, infuriating Sarah further.

"Okay," he said, "I'll go over everything we went over to revamp their team. I don't know if they'll use it, but here's the plan. Robby bats first because he's fast and gets on base a lot without having hit the ball. As soon as he gets on first, Keith bats second and takes the first pitch."

"Why?" Sarah asked impatiently.

"Are you going to keep interrupting or listen?" Daniel smirked.

Sarah slapped his upper arm. "Don't be an ass."

"Don't interrupt, then," Daniel said.

A couple had arrived and were preparing their seats in front of Daniel and Sarah as they listened to the exchange. The man laughed. He knew Sarah, but didn't recognize Daniel. "Sarah, y'all sound like a married couple. Who's your friend?"

"Hi John," Sarah said. "This is Daniel. He's been helping Jonathan with his batting. Daniel, this is John and Mandy, Steven's parents."

John shook Daniel's hand as he commented, "You must be the guy responsible for Jonathan stealing home. Amazing play."

Daniel laughed with a bit of embarrassment, and as he reached to shake Mandy's hand he replied, "That was Jonathan's doings. We just talk about baseball. He's a quick study." Daniel noticed Mandy's long fingers and tall, athletic physique and concluded that Steven got his build and ability from her.

"Are you the one who moved Steven from third base to centerfield?" Daniel caught a bit of irritation in Mandy's voice. He also felt a slight bristle from Sarah. He would have to handle Mandy carefully. She had the demeanor of an athlete and Daniel figured she had played sports at the college level, so she considered herself an expert.

Daniel explained. "Steven has the best arm on the team and he's a natural leader. He can throw the ball home from centerfield, which can save runs. So defensively he's more valuable there. The centerfielder also controls the outfield, instructing the others whether to go hard for a ball or back up the catch allowing one outfielder to run as hard as possible and not worry about missing it. If he makes the catch, he's a hero; if he misses it his backup gets it on the bounce and throws it in, so no harm is done and no extra bases for the hitter. But it takes a strong centerfielder to make that happen. I think Steven is that person."

"Hmph," was all Mandy would say.

Daniel added, "Steven could be a very good pitcher if he had some professional training. He has the build, the arm, and the talent, just not the proper mechanics."

Still stoic, Mandy did not argue.

John broke the tension. "You seem to know a lot about baseball, Daniel. Where'd you learn? Do you play professionally?"

"My father was a professional scout after coaching at Louisville. He taught me."

"Oh. Who'd he scout for?" John quizzed.

"He was a consultant. General managers would go to him to assess a player before signing multi-million-dollar contracts. He had a gift for seeing and developing talent," Daniel said.

"I'd like to meet him sometime," John said.

Sarah answered. "Daniel's father passed away a couple of months ago."

"Oh. I'm sorry, Daniel," John said.

Daniel noted a slight softening of Mandy's attitude when she heard this. It irked him that his father's death would change her attitude toward him and not the fact that he was right in his assessment of her son. But, as Daniel's father, Joseph, would say if he were here, "Grow up son. That's reality."

"Thanks, John," Daniel said. "He was a great father, and I do miss him."

With that, they took their seats and watched as the teams finished warm-ups and began the game.

Sarah whispered to Daniel. "You didn't finish telling me why Keith is taking the first pitch and not hitting."

Daniel replied quietly trying not to engage John and Mandy. "If I tell you, can we talk about the rest during the game? Maybe we'll be able to see the strategy instead of me telling it."

"Suit yourself," Sarah said, not happy with the suggestion.

Daniel explained, "Robby is fast enough to outrun a throw to second base, so if he walks, he will steal immediately. The only danger is if Keith pops the ball up or hits into a double play. So, Keith takes the first pitch allowing Robby to steal with no danger. Now Robby's in scoring position and has taken away a double play opportunity. If Keith hits a line drive, Robby will score. If he hits a fly ball to center or right field, Robby will tag up and outrun the throw to third. If Keith hits it to the infield, they will first try to hold Robby at second, then throw to first for the force out. Robby will outrun the throw and end up on third. The first baseman has to make a perfect throw and the third baseman has to tag him for the out. I think Robby can beat those odds. That puts him on third base with one out and the third and fourth batters to bring him in. If it works, that's an easy run in the first inning, so the other team feels like they're fighting out of a hole early. That's a good psychological advantage for Jonathan's team."

John turned around. He had been listening intently. "All that just by changing one position in the lineup?" John said.

"Don't ask," Sarah said. "He's liable to tell you it's like standing an egg on its end or something smart-ass like that."

"*Touché*, Mom!" Daniel said, trying to cover his embarrassment. "But the key is to find each player's strongest asset and use it to the max. Your son's arm and leadership; Robby's speed. Doing that with the whole team can turn an average team into a winning team. Everyone isn't a star athlete, but the team as a whole can be made as strong as possible."

"So, do you think they can beat Eric's team?" John asked hopefully.

"No," Daniel said. "Sorry, but the numbers just aren't there. Dad used to say, 'Always go to the numbers. Your gut speaks loudly, but the numbers never lie.' That way you don't make emotional decisions, you make rational decisions based on the odds. Of course, odds don't tell you how one play is going to pan out, but over an entire season, they work."

"Your dad was a pretty smart guy," John said.

"I'm discovering that now that he's gone. I wish I would've seen it when he was alive," Daniel lamented.

"We all have that cross to bear, Daniel," John said.

Daniel nodded.

Eric's team was the visiting team and batted first but didn't score. Their one opportunity came with one out and a man on third—normally a guaranteed run at this level of baseball. Steven, catching a high fly ball on the run, instantly transitioned the ball to his hand and stepped into the throw, using his whole body to quickly rocket the ball toward home. Eric's player on third base was tagged up and Eric sent him home as soon as Steven caught the ball. The ball bounced once into the waiting glove of the catcher who made the tag for the third out.

Eric immediately went ballistic on his runner, following him into the dugout. "Why were you just walking to home; you're supposed to run, you idiot."

"I was running, Coach. As fast as I could," his runner tried to explain.

"Shut up and sit down," Eric retorted. "You just cost us a run and the inning. You're benched. Randy—you're in."

In the stands, John and Mandy could hear Eric's tirade. John leaned over to Mandy, "That asshole would never give credit to the other team for a good play. It's always someone else who made a mistake."

"Watch your language, John," Mandy warned.

"That was a beautiful catch, though," John said. "You know he was practicing that all morning. I've never seen him throw like that. Where'd he learn it?"

Sarah kneed John who quickly turned around. She was cocking her head toward Daniel.

"Now that makes sense," John said. "Beautiful play, Daniel!"

"It's just normal outfielder stuff," Daniel said, downplaying his role. "Dad always stressed that the ball is useless in the glove. The glove is just for stopping the ball enough to get it into the throwing hand as fast as possible. Steven did that perfectly, saving hundredths of a second. But a split second is the difference between being safe and out in baseball."

Mandy finally softened her attitude toward Daniel, happy her son had saved a run and been responsible for the third out. She didn't say anything, but Daniel could sense her demeanor change from anger to respect.

The game stayed close, but Jonathan's team was still behind after several innings. Fortunately, it looked like they were not going to get slaughtered—a real testament to their improved defense.

Jonathan finally came into the game in the fifth inning and it looked like he would get to bat in the last inning. Sarah couldn't contain her nervousness as they started the bottom of the last inning. Her legs were twitching and she was wringing a napkin into pulp. Daniel was outwardly calm, belying his excitement at watching Jonathan go to the plate.

Eric's team was three runs ahead, and Jonathan was the third batter meaning that Benjamin, Eric's son, was facing the three weakest batters on the team. As they took the field, Eric walked out toward the mound with his son, admonishing him to get these three batters out quickly so they could go home victorious.

"This will be a cake-walk, Benji," Eric said to his son. "Just throw strikes and don't walk anybody, and we'll be out of here in no time."

In the stands, Mandy turned to John. "You're right. He's an asshole!"

"Watch your language, dear," John chided, grinning.

Daniel leaned down. "Baseball's never over 'til the sweet lady sings."

John just nodded, appreciating Daniel's encouragement but knowing, as Daniel had pointed out earlier, the numbers just aren't there.

Benjamin dispatched the seventh and eighth batters with no trouble, bringing Jonathan, the last batter in the lineup, to the plate with two outs.

Eric stepped out of the dugout and hollered at Benjamin. "Just three strikes, Benji. Nothing fancy! Let's get this over with."

Jonathan looked up toward Daniel and smiled, indicating that he now knew what the pitches were going to be. Daniel gave him a thumb's up sign. He stepped into the batter's box and held his hand up to the umpire as he set himself perfectly, then gripped the bat as Daniel had taught.

"Play ball!" the umpire called.

Benjamin wound up and threw a perfect strike down the middle. Jonathan moved into the pitch as he rotated his hips and moved his head with the ball. He checked his swing and watched as the ball buried itself in the catcher's mitt.

"Strike one," the umpire called.

A fan in front of John stood up to yell something, then looked around, and seeing Daniel, he nodded in recognition and sat back down, then yelled, "Let's go kid! You can do it!"

Daniel smiled.

"Why didn't he swing?" Sarah asked.

"He's getting his timing. Patience, Sarah. He's fine," Daniel said.

Jonathan watched as the second pitch went wide on the outside of the plate. The umpire called the ball and the count, "One and one."

Eric yelled from the dugout, "Strikes, Benjamin. I want to see strikes!"

Benjamin wound up and delivered a low strike. Jonathan knew there would be no extra spin on the ball, so it would come in true.

He looked for the seams, and, rotating perfectly into the ball, hit it just out in front of his body for a line drive over second base. He ran to first as he was watching the centerfielder pick it up. He rounded first and looked toward second as his base coach was telling him to stay put. Jonathan had finally gotten a real hit.

CHAPTER 13

consequences

"Time, Ump!" Eric yelled as he stormed out of the dugout toward the pitcher's mound. As he was approaching the foul line, the umpire tried to remind him he didn't have time out until granted it, and if he crossed the foul line he would be ejected from the game.

"Shut up, Roger, I called time!" He continued toward the mound, ignoring the umpire's ejection command. "Look, if you want to continue umpiring here, just shut up and get back to the plate."

Roger shot back, "Coach, either you leave or I leave; I've had enough of your crap!"

Eric ignored him as he got to the mound, intent on blasting his son.

Roger called his own son, Don, who was umpiring in the field, and together they headed for the gate. "Softball pays better anyway, Don. We can work those games and leave this asshole to his own delusions of grandeur!"

Eric got in his son's face and started haranguing, "What the hell are you throwing out here, Benjamin? Watermelons? That kid can't hit squat, and you just let him hit it to center field! I can't believe this. He's struck out every time he's ever been at bat, and all of a sudden you let him hit!"

Benjamin kept his head down and said nothing. He hated his father and hated baseball, but he had to do it or Eric would blame his mother. She would beg him to play to please Eric and Benjamin just couldn't say no.

Eric couldn't stand that his son wouldn't stand up to him. Benjamin just looked at the ground and didn't speak. Eric's fury exploded and he told Benjamin to get off the field, then looked at his bench. "Jesse, you're pitching! Get out here on the double!"

From the stands, Daniel watched incredulously, fighting to contain his anger. Jonathan stood on first base, listening as Benjamin got blasted. Jonathan could see that the first hit in his life had caused an uproar, and Daniel was livid that Eric had so marred what should have been a great moment for Jonathan. *This is exactly what's wrong with youth baseball*, Daniel thought. He could hear Joseph's voice:

"There're only two things wrong with youth baseball, Trip—parents and coaches. But the kids are great; they are what keep us going. Look at them: they just lost and they're having a blast eating their snacks and rough-housing. Kids are great. I bet they won't remember the score when they get home, but the parents will. Look at them over there. Parents and coaches arguing with the poor umpire who couldn't get off the field fast enough. They act like it's their win or their loss and the World Series is riding on this game. What idiots!"

"But Dad, you're always teaching us how to win. Isn't that important?"

"Oh, my dear Trip. We play to win since that's the objective, and so we train and practice to win. But what's the main objective?"

"I dunno."

"Fun, Trip, FUN. If it's not fun, what's the point? Never forget that! And one other secret, Trip: winning is fun!"

Daniel started down the bleachers to catch the umpires and try to defuse this fiasco. Suddenly his shoulder felt funny, and he shrugged, ignoring the feeling as he hurried to the gate to catch the umpires. His father's voice filled Daniel's memory of his last meeting with his father.

Daniel remembered during the meeting how impatient he was to get away so he could sulk and brood, his way of dealing with poor performance and the loss of Mishael. But his father did not let him out of that conference quietly.

Daniel wondered what his father was trying to remind him of now. Still hurrying toward the umpires, he knew he had to do something for Jonathan.

"Ump!" Daniel called as he raced after him. "Ump, can we talk?"

The umpire stopped and turned when he recognized Daniel's voice. Daniel began pleading with him and his son to return and finish the game. "Let me handle Eric, Blue," as umpires are affectionately called sometimes. "I promise I'll take care of him, but please finish the game for Jonathan's sake. This is his first hit, and I'd hate to see this game end this way."

"Daniel, the coach told me how much you've done for Jonathan, and it was great to see him get that hit. And what you've done for the team is remarkable. And if it was anyone else, I'd keep walking. But just for you, we'll finish. Just keep your promise about handling Eric."

"I will. I promise I will! Thanks."

• • •

Eric was stomping back to the dugout as Roger and Don came back onto the field. Eric smiled crookedly as he got his wicked way again, then looked over and caught Daniel's glance. Some of the pleasure he felt melted, but he shook it off and yelled to his players, "I want an out here or everyone does laps after the game! Play ball!"

"That's for me to say, Coach!" Roger shouted as he threw a new ball to Jesse so he could throw his warm-up pitches.

Daniel climbed the bleachers toward Sarah, still seething but exuding a feigned calm. Sarah was talking before he sat down.

"God, I'm glad Eric's bullshit didn't end the game—for Jonathan's sake. I can't believe that hit! Well, I can, but you know what I mean. I can't thank you enough for helping him. I'm so excited for him I can't stand it, and I can't quit talking. I know I'm jabbering, but I'm just so excited for him!"

"Oh, I didn't do much," Daniel responded. "He's a good kid to coach and listens and practices. The biggest thing I did was teach him to watch the ball. That's mostly it."

"You're full of it, Daniel, and you know you did wonders with his swing. Hell, I didn't even know how to buy him a bat, and his coach never even looked at him. You got him that hit, Daniel, and you'll never convince me otherwise. I watched!"

"Remember, Sarah, it's *his* hit. He worked for it, and he got it. Now you'll see why he's batting last. He's on base with the strongest part of the lineup behind him. They've got the best chance to bring him in. And Eric, to punish his son, just pulled his best pitcher and put in a weak one. Dad would call that coaching by emotions. Pretty stupid."

Daniel watched for a moment as Jesse warmed up. It wasn't pretty. Jonathan's coach glanced up toward Daniel who ran his fingers across the brim of his hat, then turned his hat around and looked at Jonathan. Jonathan nodded.

"What's all that about?" Sarah asked, noticing the ritual.

"I just told the coach to have Robby take the first pitch," Daniel explained. "Jonathan's going to steal second. With Jesse pitching, there's no way they can throw him out."

"Oh," Sarah said. "I thought you weren't going to coach from the stands anymore," she admonished.

"This was the coach's idea. We worked out some signals to use if he wanted help. He signaled me and I indicated what I would do," Daniel said.

"Oh, okay," Sarah said as they watched Jesse continue with his designated warm-up pitches.

"By the way, Sarah," Daniel asked, "is it too late to sign up for the tennis tournament?"

"You mean 'The Eric Show' at the club?"

"Is that the new name for it?"

"That's what some of us in the backroom call it. He's such a cocky bastard! Sorry, I sometimes forget he's your studio partner."

"We don't interact much. I mostly stay out of his way. He treats Jennifer like crap, which pisses me off, but I'm still the new kid, and the emphasis is on *kid*; I stay out of the fray. So? Is it too late?"

"Oh, no, it's not too late until we finish the seeding and set the brackets."

"When will that happen?"

"They're working on it now, but it won't be final until just before the tournament."

"If I sign up, can you put me in a bracket opposite Eric?" Daniel asked.

"Do you have a ranking?"

"A USTA ranking?"

"Yes," Sarah said. "Eric's in the top flight, so you'll have to play at that level to be opposite of him. Do you play tennis?"

"I've played some. Can you get me in opposite him?" Daniel asked.

"Sure. But Eric's good. He always reaches the finals and he relishes destroying everyone along the way. There are two players who can give him a run for his money if he has a bad day."

"Put them on my side then, if you can," Daniel said.

"Whatever. Consider it done. What's your charity going to be?"

"Don't we need a new field here? One with a real press box and good lights and comfortable bleachers and sunken dugouts?"

"Dream on, Daniel," Sarah said, rolling her eyes.

"That's my charity. Do you have the number for the baseball commissioner? And don't even start to tell me it's Eric."

"No, thankfully. Bill Morrison has been running the league for about fifteen years now. Nice guy. Hates Eric, but can't do anything about his attitude. I'll introduce you to him after the game. He'll be tickled to death for the help."

"Would it be okay to get Jennifer to help me with a charity contract?"

"She works for you and your associates, so do what you want. She might work after hours for you for a charity gig. She's great for that."

"Maybe I'll just pay her overtime."

"She'd love it. She could use the money. Last year Eric stiffed her for her bonus, so this year is tight for her."

"You've got to be kidding me. What did Victor say?"

"He stays out of that. On purpose. Wants the group to have that level of autonomy. Personally, I think he was upset. His rules, though, and he follows them, too. But there was a bright side to it."

"Oh?"

"Yeah. Carl Sessoms quit, or at least moved to Oregon and into another of Victor's companies because of it, so it opened up a spot for you. Lucky man you are," she paused, then added, "I think."

Daniel heard the umpire say, "Play ball," and the game continued. Jesse's first pitch was a slow strike which Robby let go by as Jonathan ran to second. The throw from the catcher was also slow, and he got to second base standing up.

Eric let out an uproar from the dugout blasting his team for being slow and lazy.

Jesse got the ball for his second pitch which was just as slow and not near the plate. Jonathan had taken a large lead, but without a steal sign from Daniel, he returned to second.

Robby let the third pitch go by, jumping out of the way as it almost hit him. The count was now two balls and one strike. Jonathan stayed on second.

"Why aren't you letting Jonathan steal?" Sarah asked.

"Not worth the risk," Daniel said. "He's in scoring position and taking a large lead, so any good hit will score him."

"Oh," she said. "You have an answer for everything, don't you?"

Daniel looked over at her quizzically. She smiled and raised one eyebrow. He loved that look. "It's called coaching, Sarah."

"I know," she said.

The next pitch was wild and the catcher missed it. Jonathan immediately ran to third. The count was now three balls and one strike.

Daniel stroked the brim of his hat as the coach looked up at him. The coach rubbed his right forearm as Robby was looking to him for instructions. Robby stepped back into the batter's box and took the next pitch. It was a ball and he threw his bat toward the dugout and ran to first.

Eric came bounding out of the dugout calling time. Roger ignored him and looked up at Daniel. Daniel mouthed a "thank you" as Roger called time.

"That was the most miserable pitching I've ever seen, Jesse. All we need is one lousy out and look what you do. Get back to the dugout."

Eric looked around for another pitcher, but knew no one else was available. He was stuck with eating crow and putting Benjamin back on the mound. He called his son out of the dugout.

Roger called to Eric, "As a returning pitcher, he's only allowed three warmup pitches, coach."

"I know, Roger," Eric said insultingly, then turned to his son. "Get me an out! Understand?"

"Yes, sir," Benjamin said quietly.

"And get some guts about you. You're such a momma's boy!"

Benjamin was seething, but remained quiet. He picked up the ball for his warmups.

Daniel watched as the coach looked up at him. Daniel stroked the brim of his hat.

Sarah saw the sign and questioned it. "Why are you having him take a pitch?"

"Same as before, but this time Robby can stroll to second if he wants," Daniel said.

"Why?" Sarah asked.

"If they throw to second, Jonathan will steal home. They won't take that chance so they'll just give Robby the base."

The catcher called time and walked to the mound, calling the shortstop in as well. After a short conference, the shortstop went toward to his position, but stopped short and stayed on the grass.

"What's that all about?" Sarah asked.

"It's a trick play," Daniel explained. "They know Robby is going to go to second and there's nothing they can do about it. So the catcher is going to act like he's throwing to second, hoping Jonathan will take the bait and try to steal home. But instead of throwing to second, he'll throw to the shortstop who is much closer. The shortstop will immediately throw it back and if Jonathan is running, they'll get him out."

"You think it will work?"

"Not a chance," Daniel said.

"Why?"

"Because they've told the world what they plan by having a conference and the shortstop already in position. Stupid. A good coach would have taught his catcher to set up the play by signaling the pitcher so the shortstop can see the signal. The shortstop waits until the pitch is thrown, then runs toward home and they make the play."

"Oh," Sarah said.

"Is 'oh' all you can say today?" Daniel laughed.

"No," she responded. "I can also say, 'up yours,'"

John turned around, grinning. "Now children," he chided.

Sarah kneed him in the back and told him to mind his own business. Mandy finally laughed, enjoying the friendly banter.

Benjamin threw a strike, Robby ran to second, and Jonathan held on third. The shortstop caught the ball and just tossed it back to Benjamin.

Daniel put his hands on his head and held them there. The coach nodded and signaled to Keith to hit away.

"Here we go," Daniel said. "This is the critical pitch of the game."

Sarah grabbed Daniel's knee to find some comfort. Daniel put his hand over hers to try and calm her down. Neither looked at the other—they were concentrating on the pitch.

Benjamin threw a perfect strike and Keith hit a hard shot to the shortstop. Out of habit, the shortstop turned toward third base to keep Jonathan from trying to score, instead of immediately throwing to first for the third out. Jonathan danced on and off the bag faking a run and buying precious time for Keith. By the time the shortstop realized his mistake and made the throw to first, it was too late. Keith beat the late throw and was safe on first to load the bases.

Eric exploded, screaming at his entire team for their ineptitude. "Now just get the easy out," he yelled. "Get the ball and touch any base! No errors!"

Benjamin took the ball and waited for Steven to come to the plate. Steven's father noticed his bat and turned to Daniel. "That's not Steven's bat. Where'd he get that one?"

"It's borrowed. His is too small for him," Daniel said.

"What do you mean? We paid almost $300 for his bat! The guy at the sport store recommended it!"

"Sorry," Daniel said. "It's not the right bat for him. Maybe it was the most profitable one for the store to sell. Has Steven grown much this season?"

"He's going through a growth spurt," Mandy admitted. "I had to buy new cleats last week."

"I didn't know that," John said to Mandy.

"Your son's growing fast, John. Better not blink, he'll be taller than you soon," Mandy warned with a smile.

"Dang. I hope it works," John said and turned to watch his son bat.

With the bases loaded, two outs, and three runs behind, Steven was the winning run if he could score. Eric's team just needed to field the ball and get it to any base for a force out, and the game would be over.

Steven set himself in the batter's box and concentrated on the pitch.

Benjamin started with a curve ball to the outside corner and Steven swung at it and missed for strike one. Benjamin tried it again hoping to get Steven to swing at a bad pitch, but Steven checked his swing and the ump called a ball, outside, for a count of one and one. Benjamin then threw a change-up inside causing Steven to swing early for strike two. The count was now one ball and two strikes. With just one more strike needed to win the game, Benjamin was in control, so he knew he could waste a pitch trying to catch Steven off-guard. He threw a fastball inside, but Steven leaned back, not taking the bait to swing, and the umpire called a ball.

Eric berated the umpire, calling him blind as a bat. Roger ignored the dig. Benjamin was furious with his dad now. He knew he would have to throw a perfect strike, or Roger would call a ball just to spite Eric.

Benjamin threw a perfect strike down the middle and Steven hit it squarely sending it high between center and left field. As it cleared the fence the stands erupted in pandemonium and watched as Steven rounded the bases and came in for the winning run. The dugout emptied and piled on top of him in celebration for hitting a grand slam to win the game.

Eric stayed in his dugout yelling at his son as the teams lined up to pass each other and shake hands.

As the fans settled down and gathered their belongings, Daniel said to John, "That's a classic example of how bad coaching can lose a game."

"I was thinking just the opposite, Daniel," John replied. "I was thinking that's a great example of how good coaching can win a game. Have you ever considered coaching?"

"No. I'm too young. Those kids need some maturity out there, not me."

"I couldn't disagree more," John said. "What they really need is someone who can teach them. Think about it, and thank you for your help. This is a game I don't think I'll soon forget."

"I'll think about it. Glad you had a good time. It was nice to meet you and Mandy," Daniel said.

Mandy reached out her hand to Daniel and Daniel responded. Her handshake was warm and firm. "Thank you, Daniel," she said.

Daniel just shrugged and said, "Steven's a good player."

He and Sarah followed John and Mandy down the bleacher steps to join in the team's celebration. Jonathan ran up to Daniel and jumped on his back. Daniel started running around acting like a bronco until they both ended up on the ground. Sarah stood over them shaking her head. "Boys! Behave yourselves!"

Daniel didn't see the rest of the team bring the water cooler up. They got both him and Jonathan with the ice-cold water, and Sarah ended up almost as wet from the splash. It was a good ending to a memorable game.

• • •

As they walked toward the parking lot, they noticed Bill Morrison standing beside a patrol car talking to a police officer.

"What's up, Bill?" Sarah asked.

"Some guy was just sitting out here in his car. Apparently, he doesn't have any kids in the league, but just wanted to sit in a parking lot and vegetate. Officer Grant took care of him. I don't think he'll be parking here anymore," Bill said.

"Was he doing anything wrong?" Daniel asked.

"Well, a man alone in a car at a youth baseball park raises red flags, you know," Bill explained. "We had a pedophile stalking the park several years ago, so now I check the parking lot every game and report anything suspicious. He was definitely suspicious. An officer questioned him and ran a check on his license. Apparently, he's from Arizona—here on business and was just looking for a place to relax between meetings. He found out that a youth park is not the place."

"Well, thanks for looking out for us, Bill," Sarah said. "By the way, I'd like to introduce you to Daniel Furman. He has an interesting proposition for you. I'll let him tell you about it while I get Jonathan and pack the car. No hurry—y'all get to know each other. I have a feeling you're going to be spending a lot of time together."

Daniel shook Bill's hand as they said the necessary clichés of introductions, then Daniel started telling him about his charity idea.

Sarah moved to the opposite side of the parking lot and as soon as she was out of earshot, called Victor.

"What's up, Sarah?" Victor asked. "You rarely call me on Saturday, so something must have you concerned. Is everything all right?"

"I don't know," Sarah said, not hiding her concern. "We're at Lockwood Park and Bill Morrison just had a man removed from the parking lot who was just sitting in his car. He apparently has no kids here. It just struck me as very strange since Daniel's here with me."

"Did they get an ID on him?" Victor asked.

"Bill said the police ran his ID. He's from Arizona, apparently just here on business. It sounded fishy to me."

"I'll get Jeffrey to pull the police report and we'll see if there's anything to it. Thank you, Sarah. Good instincts, as always, and I appreciate you watching out for the kid."

Sarah looked around as she hung up, hoping Daniel hadn't seen her making the call. He was still engaged with Bill, so she packed the car and moved closer to the pair and waited. Jonathan came up and was immediately impatient to go get a pizza.

"What are they talking about, Mom?" Jonathan asked testily.

"Maybe Daniel will get you a new batting cage if you're polite and sit still," Sarah admonished.

"Cool!" Jonathan said. "Daniel's a neat guy. You sure y'all can't date?"

"Jonathan!"

"Oh, Mom, chill out. I won't say anything about how you look at him. I know you like him."

"Jonathan, I'm going to strangle you if you say one more word!"

Jonathan laughed as he pulled his hat down over his eyes and laid his head back on the seat. "Jus' sayin'," he whispered.

CHAPTER 14

reentering the game

"Hello, is Phillip Rogers there?" Daniel asked over the phone.

"This is Phillip Rogers."

"Hi, Mr. Rogers, this is Daniel Furman."

"Who?"

"Daniel Furman, Joseph Furman's son."

"Oh! Trip! How're you doing, kid? I didn't recognize your name."

"Oh sorry, I've been going by Daniel for a while now."

"Well, I guess I'll always know you as Trip. Sorry to hear about Joseph. Are you doing okay?"

"Yes, sir. I'm doing fine. I'm living in Houston now, in Dad's condo. I found your number among his contacts. Are you still in Galveston?"

"Yep. Still at Galveston Racquet Club. Going on thirty years now. How can I help you?"

"Well, Mr. Rogers—"

"Call me Phillip, please," he interjected. "And I'll try to get used to Daniel, but no promises."

"Thanks, Mr. R,—I mean, Roger—I mean, Phillip! Daniel works a little better in the business world."

"I'm sure it does. You were asking?" Phillip prodded.

"Yes, sir. I was wondering if I could come out and hit some balls. I need to work on my game some and was hoping you had someone there who could hit with me?"

"Rice is prepping for a clay court series for the next couple weeks, and they're practicing here. I'm sure I could get one of their players to hit with you."

"I need someone who can hit fifty or sixty balls consistently with some good pace," Daniel said.

"That would be Andersen. He's their number three player. Doesn't have a kill shot, but plays like a backboard. Deep and hard, but no massive top spin. Just waits for his opponent to make a mistake. He'll never get better than the number three slot with that game, though."

"That's what I need. Who's their number one this year?" Daniel asked.

"Gary Richardson. Cocky freshman from Southern California. All he has are kill shots and no discipline. Pretty talented and pulls off some amazing wins. I don't know that he will stay in the program long. His parents are moving to England and want him to go to school there. His dad has dual citizenship, and I'm pretty sure Gary does, too."

"Andersen sounds like who I need. I don't have the time or patience for a showman," Daniel said.

"I think it will work out well for both," Phillip replied. "They have one player out with a torn Achilles. I don't think he'll ever be back, so they need a fill-in to even things out until they figure out who will replace him. They're here from four to eight daily. When did you want to come?"

"I can't make it before six, but the six-to-eight time slot would work great."

"Their coach pulls them at seven-thirty to go over films and talk about their opponents, but that will give you an hour and a half anyway," Phillip said.

"That'll work out great. I can work on serves at seven-thirty. Thanks, Mr. R . . . I mean, Phillip."

"No problem, Daniel. Will you be starting tomorrow?" Phillip enquired.

"Yes, sir."

"See you then. I'm looking forward to seeing you. How's your mom, by the way?"

"Fine. We can catch up tomorrow. Thanks again."

"Bye, Joseph—I mean, Daniel. Man, you sound like your dad."

"I hear that a lot. Bye."

Daniel hung up and stared at the phone. He was breaking an oath he made with himself never to play competitively again. *Too bad,* he thought. *It was a childish oath anyway. And pointless.* He was actually getting excited about getting back on the court.

Daniel was curious to see this Gary kid. He knew Phillip never liked anything or anyone from California, as he was Texas born and bred. But he ran a great club and superb program, one that attracted tennis aficionados from around the world. So, Daniel took what Phillip said about Gary with a big grain of salt. He would find out quickly if Gary had reason to be cocky, or if his California culture just rubbed Phillip the wrong way. Daniel dozed off thinking about it.

CHAPTER 15

schedules

"Hi, Sarah. It's Daniel. Star two fourteen really works," Daniel said as he pushed the speaker button on his office phone and Sarah's voice came to life.

"That's what it's there for, Daniel. How can I help our new Wonder Boy?"

"Sounds like you've heard something about me," Daniel said.

"First the Hudson Building, and now Trans Gulf Petroleum," Sarah replied. "News like that gets to Victor rather quickly, which means it gets to me. Congratulations! Eric must be foaming at the mouth over you!"

Daniel took the phone off speaker and picked up the receiver, sensing this phone call may take a direction he did not want to be overheard. "Maybe. I don't know. I steer clear of him. He had another row with Jennifer yesterday. I swear I don't know how she puts up with him."

"How's she doing with you?" Sarah asked.

"Great. She's amazing. She knows what I need before I ask for it and keeps me organized. She gets me so prepared for meetings it's incredible."

"Sooo, what can I do for you?" Sarah asked.

"I need to rearrange my schedule with Jonathan for a few days."

"Work getting in the way? I understand." Her voice had a tone of condolence.

"No, it's not that. Work's busy and getting busier, but I just need to work with him earlier, and I know you're not able to get him to the cage before five."

"That's not what I was expecting to hear," she said. "I figured you would drop him now that your work was taking off."

Daniel detected the up-tick in her attitude. "Why would you think that? You don't know me very well after all, do you?"

"Sorry. I deserved that," Sarah confessed. "I just haven't had much experience with men who actually do what they commit to, so I assume the worst."

"That's too bad. We're not all cretins, you know," Daniel chuckled. "Although I can't say I have too many stellar qualities, as I'm sure you'll learn if you're around me very long."

"Don't sell yourself short and don't try to bullshit me," Sarah shot back. "I hear the talk around the water coolers, to use a cliché. The young women in this building are dying to get to know you, and they pump Jennifer for any tidbit of info she will drop."

"And what does she say?" Daniel asked, trying to contain his impatience.

"Nothing. Absolutely gives up nothing. She's got your back, and she's very professional. But if there's anyone you want to get to know, she's your source."

"I'll keep that in mind," Daniel said, wanting to get on with the real conversation. "Now, about Jonathan. Can I pick him up from school and take him to the cage and have you get him by five-thirty? I need to be in Galveston by six."

"Hot date?"

"Yeah, I wish, but no. Just an appointment."

"Really? It's not on your calendar," Sarah said.

"Do you know everything in this company? No privacy at all?"

"Excuse me," Sarah said churlishly, "but Victor knows everything and has access to everything, so all calendars are linked to his computer and mine. He can tap in whenever and wherever he wants. And, for the record, he's been very impressed with your work so far. He's really intrigued with the total building management concept you've been putting together since your first meeting with him. I'm sure that's what sealed the deal with TGP. He may have you revamp some of our older contracts and infuse some new blood into the system."

"He hasn't mentioned anything like that to me!" Daniel was surprised and elated since he had been worried about Victor's silence.

"He will, in due time. He asked me to talk to you about it if I ran into you. Consider yourself prepped for your next fifteen minutes with him."

"Okay, great. When?" Daniel asked, trying to show his excitement.

"Tomorrow morning."

"What time?"

"Six-fifteen."

"Perfect," Daniel said.

"Perfect? Are you serious? So, the rumors are true?" Sarah commented.

"Rumors?" Daniel was puzzled.

"You start your day at five a.m.?"

"Most days, yes."

"When do you sleep?"

"At night?" Daniel said, half as a question and half as a statement, implying the obvious nosiness of her questions.

"Of course, of course. It's just that I know you weren't back from Galveston until after eleven last night, and you were here at four-thirty," Sarah said.

"Are you stalking me, Sarah?"

"No, silly. Victor had a group of investors he wanted you to meet last night so he went by your condo and talked to the doorman. Harold, right?"

"Yes. Harold."

"Harold said you weren't in."

"He's not supposed to give out personal info—"

"Oh, he didn't," Sarah replied before Daniel finished his sentence. "Victor couldn't get any more out of him except a promise to ask you to call him if you came in by eleven. You didn't call, so Victor asked Ramon to buzz him when you came in this morning. Ramon was scared to buzz Victor at four-thirty, but did it anyway, so I heard about it when Ramon quizzed me this morning to find out if he was in trouble for waking up Victor."

"Well, that explains Ramon's curiosity this morning," Daniel said. "He rarely says anything to me, but this morning he was as talkative as a mynah bird, and nervous."

"I guess nervous about calling Victor, and inquisitive in case Victor started asking questions. But he didn't . . . So, no hot date in Galveston and nothing on your calendar?"

"Are you prying again, Sarah?"

"Just having a little fun with you. Don't get your feathers ruffled. We older folks have to live vicariously through you young bucks, you know."

Daniel laughed, enjoying Sarah's playful nature.

"Seriously, Daniel, when do you sleep?"

"Seriously, Sarah," Daniel chided, "I sleep four hours a night. That's all I can sleep. My father didn't require much sleep either. It drove my mom nuts. The only time I slept more than four hours was as a teenager. When most teens needed twelve hours of sleep, I slept six. Mom can still sleep until noon on Saturdays, so you can imagine she was fit to be tied when I would wake her up at six in the morning asking for breakfast. Finally, I learned to take care of myself at night, and really enjoyed having the world to myself. It's amazing what you can do when nobody is around to distract you. It really paid off in college, though. I don't know how other athletes do it. Of course, I never had tutors, but I had to maintain a B average, in engineering no less, to keep my scholarship."

"So, you made B's in college?"

"One."

"One? You mean otherwise you made all A's? All the way through college?" Sarah tried to sound surprised, but she knew Daniel's school performance.

"Yes," Daniel said quietly, now embarrassed that he sounded like a braggart.

"So, what was the B in? Advanced meta-astro-physics or something?"

"No, it was construction law. Best grade I ever got, too."

"How was a B better than all those A's?"

"Well, not to bore you with the facts, ma'am, but if you must know, I learned a huge lesson from that B."

"How so?"

"A lot of construction law deals with specifications, and being in civil engineering, we learn a lot about construction and buildings and such. So, one of the most common mistakes spec writers make is using the word *should* instead of *shall*."

"What's the difference?" Sarah asked.

"Actually, it's a huge difference. *Should* implies a choice, like you don't have to do it, such as *the contractor should proof-roll the sub base prior to paving*."

"I don't know what that is, but I get the implication," Sarah said.

"What it means is the contractor *should* do it but isn't obligated to do it. If you say the contractor *shall* proof-roll, then it's a command, and he is contractually bound to that action."

"And the B, Daniel?" Sarah's curiosity making her impatient with the long answer.

"Well, the final exam was rewriting a paragraph of specifications, which I did with great enthusiasm, examining it sentence by sentence and rewording the entire paragraph, when all the professor wanted was to change *should* to *shall*, which, during the careful rewriting, I left in. It was a classic case of not seeing the forest for the trees. I was so focused on the task, I missed the whole, and it cost me a letter grade. So now, when I get too focused, I try to step back and see the big picture. In engineering, we sometimes focus so intently on the minutia that we miss the entire purpose. The B is a constant reminder not to lose perspective."

"That's a pretty good lesson—well worth a B, I might say. So, you sleep from twelve to four and are in here by five?"

"Generally, but it varies. I still like to run and climb the stairs in the morning, but that's becoming more of a challenge. For some reason, my twenty-hour days are packed full."

"Are you sure you have time for Jonathan?"

"Absolutely. I think I'll need a note to pick him up, won't I?"

"Yes. I'll send one down. By the way, they delivered your copy of the Palo Alto newspaper to our floor again, so I'll send it down with the note. Do you ever even read it? Jennifer says she finds it in the trash, looking as if it hasn't been read."

"Still being nosy, Sarah?"

"I guess so, my young man of mystery. Just curious about what's so intriguing in Palo Alto these days." Sarah paused and Daniel heard a phone in the background. "Gotta go. Victor is calling in. See you at five-thirty."

"Okay, thanks. Bye." Sullenness engulfed Daniel as he thought about Palo Alto and the inevitable disappointment he would feel after looking through the paper. He reclined his chair and stared at the ceiling as he waited for Sarah's note. He wondered if he would spend the rest of his life looking through the Palo Alto newspaper for a message from Mishael.

CHAPTER 16

lunch with jennifer

"What is it, Jennifer?" Daniel looked up from his desk, a large glass table perched on sawhorse-shaped supports with stools around it—higher than average desks, so he could stand or sit. He had moved out the traditional furniture and outfitted the office more to his style of working. He stood a lot and paced when on the phone or thinking, so the office had no dead-end spaces. It also had no head or foot, so anyone who came in could take any stool, sit anywhere, and feel on an equal basis. Jennifer was standing in his doorway, looking perplexed.

"Well, come in and sit down. What's the problem?"

She came in and looked around. She rarely went into the associates' offices because they either came out to her or met her in the studio conference room to go over business. She immediately felt the stark difference between Daniel's and Eric's offices. Eric's had heavy wood molding and wainscoting, integral with ornate bookshelves full of books she knew he never touched, and established a definite visual hierarchy with his large, plush chair commanding the center of attention behind his antique walnut desk. All other furniture was sized and placed subservient to his. His carpet was too thick for an efficient office, but efficiency took a back seat to the image of importance Eric craved.

Daniel's office seemed spartan by comparison. Instead of the dark oil paintings with heavy frames adorning Eric's papered walls, Daniel had two pieces of matched original works, Picasso-like in their lightness, with minimal frames and a small spotlight on each one. They hung by wires against his white walls. The wood of his desk supports and stools, as well as his one file cabinet, was natural finished birch, and contrasted nicely with the pecan flooring he installed in lieu of the carpeting. She also noticed the vinyl base trim, prevalent throughout the building, had been replaced with a simple wood base topped by a mahogany dowel forming a thin line around the room and doorway and adding a light touch of color and serenity to the space.

"Did you do this yourself, Daniel?" Jennifer asked.

"Oh, God, no. This is way out of my bailiwick. I had an architect help me. Actually, the same architect who did Dad's condo interior. I never knew he used an architect, but I always loved the condo, and it fit Dad so well. I found the drawings when I moved in, and got the architect's name there. I called him and asked if he did offices, and he was very nice and agreed to meet me on a weekend. I had never met an architect and really didn't know what to expect or how much it would cost, but I knew I didn't want the interior decorator who came with this building."

"Why not? She's free."

"Well, that just means she gets a commission on what she sells, so she wanted to fill my office and walls with everything I didn't want or need. Cheesy artwork, vases, statuettes, lamps, side tables, stuff like that."

"How was the architect?" Jennifer asked, some of her hesitation relieved by Daniel's willingness to talk.

"It was a little weird at first. He met me here early on a Saturday morning on his way to the marina. He looks like he sails a lot—suntanned face, long white hair, deck shoes without socks, shorts and

T-shirt—you know. Anyway, he looked around, sat down, and asked me to start talking. I thought he wanted me to tell him what I wanted, you know, furniture-wise, but after a few minutes he stopped me and asked me to talk about how I wanted my office to feel. That was weird. I didn't even have words for how I wanted it to feel, but he guided me and filled in words—pattern language or something like that, he called it—and sketched as I talked. He was a good listener, unlike the decorator who just talked the entire time. Anyway, I also asked that the work be done on the weekends so as not to disturb the business. He said that was no problem.

"The next week he brought in sketches and color samples, and I was amazed. It was like what wasn't here was just as important as what was here. He nailed the design, and he recommended a contractor who started work one Friday night and was done by Monday morning."

"Yeah, I remember that weekend," Jennifer said. "Amazing transformation, and you were so quiet about it no one knew you were doing an office renovation. It's really beautiful, but I really need to talk to you."

"Oh, yeah. Sorry to get sidetracked. What's wrong?"

She looked around as if seeking some privacy. "It's a personal issue."

"Hmm." Daniel looked at her with hesitation. "You know, we haven't had any time to talk, so why don't we grab lunch?"

"That's not necessary," Jennifer said nervously.

Jennifer's body language screamed otherwise, so Daniel insisted. "Have you been to Jeremy's Deli?"

"No. Haven't heard of it."

"It's a hole in the wall on the next block, but he has the best hot pastrami and Swiss I've eaten—he makes his own rye bread. And it's quiet. I haven't seen anyone from VCM there yet, so we can talk. Here's the address. I'll call for a booth. Just mention my name when you get there and Jeremy will take care of you. I'll be a few minutes behind you."

Jennifer took the note and left, excited about a lunch out of the office—a rarity for her.

She passed the door to the restaurant twice to scope it out, and then tentatively opened the door.

"You must be Jennifer," she heard immediately, as a small, rotund figure came up to her, grabbed her hand, and escorted her toward the back of the small restaurant. "Daniel called ahead. He will be here shortly. Your sweet tea is already at the table, and Daniel ordered you a club on our own marbled rye, no mayonnaise. Will that be okay with you? Our sweet potato fries are famous in the city, but we also have regular fries, potato salad, or mixed vegetables."

Jennifer was quietly amazed. She recovered from her surprise and said the sweet potato fries would be fine, and yes, the club was perfect. She sat and tasted the tea. It was the perfect sweetness, obviously real sugar. She looked up to see Daniel come in. He had put on his coat and tie and looked like a million bucks. He passed the long mirror on the wall and never even glanced toward it. *God, is he oblivious to his own looks?* she thought. *And how in the world did he know what to order for me?*

"Hey," Daniel said, sliding into the booth. "I hope the club is okay with you."

"Great," she said. "How'd you know that's my favorite sandwich?"

"I have my sources," he said, smiling.

"Right!" Jennifer said. "Well, it's good to have already ordered. I need to be back by one-thirty."

"Nope, not 'til four o'clock."

"What?"

"I called Sarah and had your schedule cleared for a long lunch," Daniel said. "If Eric says anything, he'll get a note from Victor, through Sarah, of course. I figured it was time we get to know more about one another."

"Wow. Thank you, Daniel," Jennifer said. "I can use a leisurely lunch. They are all so hurried and most days I eat at my desk. This will be lovely. And when did you find this jewel of a restaurant?"

"As I said, I have my sources," he grinned.

"Oh, a man of mystery, are we?" Jennifer cocked her head slightly, emphasizing mystery.

Daniel felt the lightening of Jennifer's demeanor and was glad he sensed her need for private counsel and a break.

"Did I tell you how impressed I am with your office?" Jennifer said.

"That means you're impressed with my architect—not me. Which is okay, since I'm impressed with him, too. He was the one who recommended the clothes consultant, too."

"If he was your father's architect, then he's also who designed Victor's homes here and at the beach. Those are beautiful homes. I never saw your father's condo, but I heard it was quite nice."

"I really enjoy it. It's small, but perfect."

"You know, I'm pretty sure he's the same architect Eric called to redo his office." Jennifer said.

"Really? Doesn't seem fitting," Daniel responded.

"Oh, he met with Eric, then wrote a note declining the commission and recommending another architect," Jennifer confided. "Eric was incensed. Never called the other guy. Got some fraternity brother from UVA to come down and redo it."

Daniel shrugged without commenting, inwardly relieved he and Eric had not used the same architect.

Jeremy brought the food, having taken it from their server to deliver it himself. When he placed Daniel's plate on the table, he leaned down and whispered in Daniel's ear, "Do you know the man in the front booth?"

Daniel glanced up and saw a well-dressed, Middle Eastern-looking man about forty. He didn't recognize him. "No. Never seen him before. Why?"

"He's been here every time you have, so I was just wondering. Thought you might know who he is."

"Sorry," Daniel shrugged.

Jennifer picked up her sandwich. She paused, noticing Daniel touched his fingers to his forehead for a moment to offer a quick, silent blessing before picking up his hot pastrami. *This guy is full of surprises,* she thought, and then realized his little surprise was probably going to make her conversation even more difficult. She decided to eat and let him start the conversation.

"The sauce they give you for the sweet potato fries is unbelievable," Daniel said as he reached across to help himself to a fry dipped in the sauce. She then noticed he opted for a Caesar salad with his sandwich. *Another little enigma,* she thought.

"I was wondering what that was," she said, trying the sauce. *He was right. It's to die for.*

"So, what's on your mind, Jennifer?" he asked.

"I'm sorry to have to talk to you about this, Daniel, and I know what a private person you are, but rumors are flying around the office, and they seem to land in my lap. It's gotten to the point I just don't know how to handle them and protect your privacy. I'm in a quandary about whether or not to even talk to you about it, so please don't be upset with me, and if any of this is offensive to you, please just forgive me and forget."

"Jennifer, Jennifer," Daniel interrupted. "Slow down. Just tell me about the rumors, and I'm sure we can handle them. I know you've got my best interest at heart, so talk to me. I'm a big boy; don't be shy."

Jennifer took a breath. "Well, the problem is, Daniel, that, well, you've got to know you are the . . . this sounds so cheesy."

"Spit it out, Jen," Daniel said as he coaxed a piece of Swiss cheese into his mouth along with a large slice of pastrami.

"Okay. You've got killer looks and there are a lot of single—and married—women in the building wondering about you; and you've been here for a while now and nobody has seen you go out with anyone or show any interest in anyone—except for Sarah—and she insists y'all are strictly friends, no dating. And then, all of a sudden, a rumor started flying around that you're gay. Nobody has seen you show any interest there either, but there's still the rumor, and I don't know how to stop it or even respond or protect you, and the rumor started after you landed the TGP contract, so it's possible Eric started it because I know he's super pissed at you and wants you to fail, but I'm not sure and . . ." Jennifer couldn't seem to slow down.

"Jennifer. Slow down," Daniel swallowed, then continued. "First of all, I am not gay. And I don't think it should be an issue one way or the other, but—"

"Well, Eric is homophobic," Jennifer interrupted.

"I am not gay," Daniel repeated. "I don't care what Eric thinks. He's got his own issues, and I'm not going to give any credence to him or his opinion. And I appreciate that you are trying to protect me, but I honestly don't care what people think or say about me. If they have nothing better to do than speculate on my life and my lifestyle, then all I can say is they need to get a life. I don't live my life to please their childish fantasies in any way, shape, or form. I seriously and honestly do not care. I didn't move to Houston to find a wife or a new dating scene. Quite the opposite, in fact."

"Oh?" Jennifer's curiosity was instantly piqued.

"I had a rough final semester in California, and Houston is supposed to be a sabbatical for me," Daniel said. "A healing, or a new beginning or something. I'm not exactly sure, but it's supposed to be a place where I have no baggage, no history, and no responsibilities to anyone but myself. I'm trying very hard to keep it that way. I figured I'd breeze into Houston for a year or so, get my life straight and breeze out—as empty as I arrived, with no wake, so to speak. But I'm finding that much harder than I imagined."

"Why Houston?" Jennifer asked.

"I met Victor at Dad's funeral. He took me to dinner after, and we ended up talking most of the night. I knew him as a friend of my father by name only. He told me a lot about Dad I never realized. I took so much for granted—my coaches, my education, my . . . well, everything. And Victor explained what Dad had done, without my knowledge, to facilitate so much of . . . well, of everything I thought was my own. It was overwhelming. He planted the seed that night about Houston. He told me about his friendship with Dad, too. Men of his wealth usually lose all their friends and are left with acquaintances and associates."

"Oh? Why is that?" Jennifer pressed.

"Sooner or later every friend asks for help, monetarily. If he says yes, the friendship is over because he has to collect on the debt and make a profit. If not, it's a charity case and all respect is lost, so the friendship is over. And if he says no, the friendship ends right there. According to Victor, Dad never asked him for anything. They went on a vacation together for a week every year. Victor had to hide the activity to keep it private due to his wealth, and Dad would never fly, so he would drive to Maine every year, pick Victor up at the airport, and drive into the mountains to a cabin they owned. Everything they did—the hunting, the fishing, the eating—was within Dad's budget and the expense was split fifty-fifty. Victor said those were the best vacations he ever had."

"Nobody else went?" Jennifer asked.

"There were apparently no rules except for privacy and the expenses, so I know sometimes they took girlfriends or wives, but Victor said the women usually got bored quickly, so the best vacation was when it was just the two of them. He said sometimes they would fish in the small boat all night long, and then cook their catch over an open fire on a nearby shore for breakfast. It was so rejuvenating. The world did not exist for that week. Just them and the mountains."

"So, why wouldn't your dad fly?" Jennifer asked.

"Well, I was his second family. He first married his high school girlfriend and they had two children. One year he took a coaching position in Louisville and, before making the move permanent, would fly his wife and children out there in the university president's private plane. One trip over the Appalachians the fog rolled in quickly, and they flew into a mountain. The pilot had an instrument rating but still flew them into a mountain. It took three days to find the wreckage. Dad never got in an airplane after that; if he couldn't drive or take a boat, he wouldn't go. He didn't marry again until late in life, and that wasn't really successful, except, Victor said, he got me. My mom's beautiful, but she really married Dad 'cause she thought it was romantic or something to be with an older man. But she never could let go of the attention younger men gave her. Dad let her go, but I'm sure he never fell out of love with her, and never got over his first family, either. Victor told me most of what I know about them."

"So, Victor invited you to come to Houston and start over?"

"He planted the seed, like I said, but Dad's death was just one of my issues."

"What else was going on that semester?"

Daniel took a deep breath and sat back in his seat. "Mishael was going on."

"What a beautiful name. Who was she?" Jennifer asked.

"I've talked enough about me and monopolized our time. I want to know something about you."

"I appreciate that, Daniel, and I'll be happy to tell you all about my uneventful life. But not today. This is your time, and I need to know, and want to know, more about you. Tell me about Mishael. Where is she?"

"I honestly don't know."

"What happened? Her name sounds Mediterranean," Jennifer said.

"Pakistani. Royalty. A real-live princess. And unbelievably beautiful. The olive skin, the long jet-black hair, green eyes. I would melt just looking at her. And she was very small. Barely five feet. And for her height, she had long, elegant fingers." Daniel felt awkward mentioning that.

"Fingers? You're telling me about her hands?"

"Oh, my God, her hands were the most beautiful thing about her, except they were too small."

"Too small? I thought you said her fingers were long?"

"I said long for her height, but being so small, her fingers were actually too small for the piano. You see, she was at Stanford in the music department and would have been a concert pianist, but she couldn't reach some of the keys on some of the pieces."

"That's sad," Jennifer lamented.

"Not really. She would make up other chords as a substitute, but her professors would blast her for it, calling it heresy to do that to the masters' works."

"So, what did she do?" Jennifer asked.

Daniel shrugged, giving in to Jennifer's prodding, and continued telling her about Mishael. "She ignored them. Totally ignored them. She said all they did was read music and regurgitate it. She felt music with her soul. She said the dots and lines on the sheets came alive to her and swirled in her head in a multi-dimensional world that even the piano could not fully express. I would spend my study time in the music building while she practiced, and after everyone else left, she would throw the sheets of music off the piano and start playing. She said this was our music—ours alone. It was the most beautiful music I've ever experienced. It would fill my pores. I asked her one time who wrote it and what it was called. She looked at me like I was a child, and said it was hers and her soul pouring out through the piano. It was not written anywhere. She would make it up as she played. Sometimes for hours. Just played and played.

"One time, another student came in late to practice. As soon as the door opened, Mishael's music stopped and she went into a Mozart piece as if she had been playing it all along. It was flat and lifeless compared to what she played when we were alone. I'll never hear music like that again. Ever. I know it. She used to say Beethoven could write when he was deaf because he wrote with his soul, not his ears, and the professors just read music, so she ignored them. She was accepted at Juilliard but didn't go."

"What happened? Why didn't she go?" Jennifer asked.

"Even though her father discouraged it, her high school teachers went behind her father's back and got someone from New York to come out and listen to her play. They quietly pushed her admission through, and when she got the letter, her father was incensed. They are very devout Muslims, and her father rules with an iron hand. He would not allow her away from them, especially to go to New York, unescorted and alone. It was unthinkable. She often warned me that we could not be seen together alone, so we were always in a crowd, except in the music building. That was our sanctuary. We had a place in the library on the eleventh floor where we would leave notes. We called it our *mailbox*, and we communicated that way, privately. She placed one sealed envelope there and said I was only to open it if she left me. I started to protest, but she handed me a similar envelope and asked me to write her a final message, just in case anything happened or I left her. She made me swear I would never touch the sealed envelopes unless something happened to us. We used to sleep together under the tables in the conservatory when everyone else was gone. Her family did not know about it and assumed she was practicing, so she was always out before twelve, with a taxi always waiting for her.

"One night, she fell asleep in my arms, and I didn't wake her in time. When she did wake up, long after midnight, she was frantic and very angry with me. She ran outside, but there was no taxi, just a black Mercedes waiting for her." Daniel paused, shaking his head mournfully.

"That was the last time I saw her," he said. "I wandered around the campus most of the night in a panic, then decided to go to the library. When the elevator was too slow to open, I started running up the stairs. Eleven flights and I couldn't get there fast enough. I nearly passed out at the eleventh floor and literally crawled to our mailbox, unable to get a breath. My last note to her was gone as well as my sealed envelope, but there was no reply note from her—just her sealed envelope. I ripped it open, and what it said was devastating.

"The next day, when she didn't show up for class, I went to her house, but no one would answer at the gate. I knew they were home, but after I tried for an hour to get a response, the police showed up with a restraining order against me and said I was not to come within a thousand feet of their house. It did not mention Mishael, just the residence. I tried to call, but her phone had been cut off. Back at the conservatory no one had seen her, and her locker had been cleaned out."

"Daniel! What did the note say?" Jennifer pressed.

"Basically, it said if I had honored our vow and not opened the envelope unless she had left me, then she was gone. It meant her father had found out she was seeing a Christian, and she was on her way back to Pakistan to an arranged marriage. She had always tried to warn me. She was always so careful. But I was too naive and too stupid to listen. I never imagined the absolute control her father exercised over her. She had also warned me I would probably be followed for a long time. Her father is very wealthy and can easily afford to have me watched. She said to absolutely not try to contact her, but to watch the want ads in the Sunday edition of the Palo Alto newspaper. She said to look for a 'thirty-eight-inch avocado oven' and call for it. There is no such thing as a thirty-eight-inch oven, much less in avocado."

"So that explains why we get the Palo Alto newspaper in the mail every Tuesday and I find it in the garbage, unread."

"Yes. I take out the want ads and throw the rest away."

"She took your letter? What did it say? If you don't mind me asking?"

"That's okay," Daniel said. "It was blank. I was never going to leave her."

Jennifer felt a lump in her throat. She wanted to say something, anything, but words wouldn't form. She fumbled through her purse for a tissue. She took her phone and wallet out and placed them on the seat beside her, then got the tissues and blew her nose. She just sat there watching Daniel. *No wonder it's so easy for him to ignore all the women in the building,* she thought. *They must seem like cheap gold-diggers to him after Mishael.* As she picked up her wallet, her phone slipped off the seat. It took her a moment to retrieve it off the floor. Slowly she sat back up and wiped the moisture from her eyes as she looked down, averting Daniel's eyes.

"I hate to skip out, Jennifer, but I need to pick up Jonathan at three-thirty," Daniel said.

"I thought we had 'til four?" Jennifer said, disappointed.

"You have 'til four, or later if you want. Just call Sarah, she'll cover for you." Daniel reached into his jacket pocket and took out an envelope and slid it over to Jennifer. "Jen, I know the bonus law at VCM, but I found a way around it, and I cleared it with Sarah. You've been such a huge help since I've been here, and I wanted to show my appreciation after *we* landed the TGP contract. This is a debit card, in my name, but for you. It has $1,000 on it and expires in one week, so you are to go shopping or whatever you want. Indulge yourself."

Jennifer looked down at her clothes and suddenly felt frumpy next to Daniel. *How could he ruin a perfect lunch like this?* she thought. *Men are so stupid!* She wanted to scream, but composed herself and thought, *He's just trying to be nice, and truthfully, this is one of the nicest things anyone has done for me, and I feel like crap. What is wrong with me, anyway?*

"The PIN number is there also, and the banker's name and number in case anyone questions it being in my name," Daniel continued, oblivious to her emotional welling.

"Thank you, Daniel, and thank you for lunch and for the afternoon. I don't think they brought the check, though."

"It's taken care of already."

"Can I help with the tip, then?" Jennifer offered.

"Thanks, but already done." Daniel got up to leave and waited for Jennifer to gather her phone and purse. He motioned her to go ahead and then opened the door for her. She turned around to thank him again, and he hugged her, thanking her for caring enough to watch out for him, and for all her help. She wrapped her arms around him and felt his broad chest and hard back muscles. *Not an ounce of fat on this guy,* she thought, as her knees felt like jelly. She hated him for making her feel so inadequate, but relished the attention she had been given. She wanted desperately to reach up and kiss his neck but fought the urge, knowing it would be incredibly inappropriate. She felt him release her and turn to leave. As she watched him walk away, she began thinking, *A thousand dollars on a card in his name with a week to spend it! How perfect. He must have known that any cash would have gone straight in the bank, and I would never spend it on myself. Now he will know where I spent it, what I spent it on, and it will have to be done immediately. That was very slick of him. First, I'll buy a pair of shoes and then call Sarah and find out who does her hair. It always looks so elegant and mine hangs like a mop. Daniel has no idea how far I can stretch a thousand dollars. But he's about to find out.*

She looked down the block at her building, and up to where she imagined her windows were. Then she turned and walked the other way as she took her phone out and dialed Sarah's private line.

"Hi Sarah. It's Jennifer. Is Victor available?"

"Let me check. How was lunch?" Sarah asked.

"Wonderful. Daniel's such a gentleman."

"And how was your club on marbled rye?"

"So you are his secret source. I figured as much. It was perfect."

"Always glad to help. I'll put you through to Victor."

"Thanks, Sarah," Jennifer said as she heard the phone click and Victor's voice came on the line.

"What is it, Jennifer?"

"I know why Daniel gets the Palo Alto paper."

"Great. Tell me."

"There's something else. Jeremy at the restaurant asked Daniel about a man who always seems to be there when Daniel is. Daniel didn't know him. I got a photo of him, but it's not very good. I took it with my phone from under the table and got enough of his face that I think you can check him out."

"That is interesting," Victor said. "Send it to Sarah and come see me in the morning, first thing."

"Yes, sir." Jennifer put her phone back in her purse and headed toward her favorite department store.

CHAPTER 17

andersen

"**D**aniel, this is Andersen. Andersen, Daniel Furman."

Standing on one of the freshly groomed clay courts of Galveston Racquet Club, Daniel shook Andersen's hand, immediately noticing his apathetic handshake, as Phillip finished the introductions. Obviously, Andersen was nonplussed with this chore but had resigned himself to it. As the number three player, he had to undertake some of the chores of entertaining tennis wannabes. It was hardly worth his small scholarship, but the scholarship was better than nothing so he said the necessary polite clichés and grabbed some practice balls.

"Sorry, Andersen, but I'd rather practice with new balls," Daniel said and opened up two new cans.

"Whatever you want," Andersen said, barely concealing his disdain. Daniel could finish the silent sentence Andersen left hanging, *As if new balls would really make any difference.* Daniel accepted the subtle rebuke, understanding Andersen's attitude. He had entertained his share of *weekenders*, as his father politely referred to those who aspired to be better than their potential. He always encouraged Daniel to be very polite and patient with players like that. "Tennis is a lifelong sport, Trip," he would say, "and you've been given a great gift. Learn to share it and let them dream the dream of greatness. It's all they will have. And remember, you're only great at a few things also. Everyone has their own gift, and unfortunately, yours will not last long."

Daniel sat down for a moment and retied his shoes. They did not need it, but he wanted to make sure Andersen went out onto the court first and waited for Daniel to join him.

Andersen took the bait and headed out onto the court. Daniel grinned slightly, enjoying his first small victory over Andersen. *Now let's see what this guy has,* he thought and ambled onto the court, noticing immediately the sun's position. Andersen had taken the closest court side, not the best court side from the sun's position. *Victory number two,* Daniel thought and waited for Andersen to start the warm-ups. Andersen hesitated, then hit a short ball to Daniel. Daniel returned equally in pace and position, and so the short warm-up progressed. Andersen noticed immediately the smoothness of Daniel's strokes, the seemingly effortless footwork always ending in a perfect setup for the next shot. Andersen increased his pace slightly, and Daniel returned it equally, never faster or better, but precisely. Forehand to forehand, backhand to backhand. Finally, Andersen put all of his pace onto a ball, and Daniel let it go by, indicating with one finger up the ball had gone long. Daniel had won round one with Andersen. Now he could get down to the business of getting his own game back into shape.

Although he had matched Andersen's shots, Daniel felt the tightness and rustiness of being absent from the game. After a half hour of hitting, Daniel stopped and went over to his bag. Andersen joined him, his demeanor more demure than when they had first stepped onto the court.

"Where'd you learn to play tennis?" Andersen asked.

"Florida."

"College?" Andersen asked.

"Played in Gainesville," Daniel replied, purposely downplaying the question as he shuffled through his bag.

"University of Florida," Andersen stated.

Daniel nodded and began pulling a camera and tripod out of his bag. "Mind if I set this up?" Daniel asked, knowing the permission was totally unnecessary but asking nonetheless.

"Why the camera?" Andersen quizzed.

"I don't have the luxury of a coach, and I haven't hit in a while, so I want to see how I'm doing."

"You look pretty good to me, but I'm no coach. Are you prepping for a tournament or something?"

"Or something," Daniel said. He was almost finished setting up the camera and was anxious to get back on the court.

"Are you a pro somewhere?" Andersen asked, trying to get some more information out of Daniel.

"No. I work for VCM in their property management division in downtown Houston," Daniel said nonchalantly.

"Oh. Money must be pretty good, huh?"

"It's okay. Can we get back to hitting?" Daniel purposely showed impatience with the questions.

"Sure. What did you say your last name was?"

"Furman," Daniel said, hoping to end the conversation.

"Wasn't there a Trip Furman who played out in California? Any kin to you?"

"Might be a distant cousin," Daniel lied.

"Yeah, I think he's a lot younger too."

"Can we play now?"

Daniel was barely able to contain his amusement at how he had been able to appear older just by getting rid of the carefree college student look and adopting the hairstyle, clothes, and demeanor of an executive. Shaving every day was a real drag, and he hated the once-a-week haircuts, done as close to high and tight as he could bear without looking military. His new country club tennis attire was a stark contrast to Andersen's ragged shorts and T-shirt, complete with an advertisement for a local beer joint. It seemed almost comical to Daniel that he had so quickly attuned to his new look. Although he shouldn't have been, he was always surprised at the respect he commanded downtown whenever he went out on business ventures or luncheons, dressed in one of his new suits, starched shirts, silk ties—tied with a perfect dimple—and polished Italian leather shoes. He had also indulged himself with five pairs of glasses with photochromic lenses that had the benefit of acting as sunglasses but had no corrective value. He had gone through his dad's clothes when he moved into the condo, hoping to save some money by using them, but everything was dated or worn out, so he took it all to the local thrift store and called a clothes consultant to help with his wardrobe. He was shocked at how little he knew about men's fashion and how much he learned from the consultant. Even jewelry, which he hated, had its place in the understated, but complete, closet. An understated but nice ring, a proper watch, a lapel pin and cufflinks—all coordinated with the glasses' frames—made him feel complete. He drew the line at the manicure and clear polish suggested by his consultant, who had quickly agreed with him.

"Most executives opt for that," he'd said, "thinking it is a sign of wealth, but it is still cheesy to me and highly unnecessary. Just keep your nails neat so you don't look like you've been gardening."

Daniel had gone back to the consultant for a line of casual clothes, and in the end ditched every thread he brought from California. He could not believe how expensive clothes could be, nor how beneficial. He had never had them fit so well or look so naturally correct. And, unknowingly, Andersen had just put the icing on the cake for him.

• • •

They continued to hit for another hour, Daniel giving Andersen specific instructions about the drills he wanted to run, and Andersen complying without question, his respect for Daniel growing with each series of hits. Finally, Daniel stopped and queried, "Aren't you supposed to be watching films or something now?"

"Oh crap! What time is it? Dammit, if I'm late, Coach McKenzie will ream me. He loves to make a spectacle of anyone who walks in late."

"Sorry. I thought you were keeping track of the time," Daniel said.

"No. It's not your fault. This was a great session. I was really into it and lost all concept of the time. Are we on for tomorrow also?" Andersen asked hopefully.

"Sure. That will be great, if it's okay with Lloyd."

Daniel purposely called Coach McKenzie by his first name, further cementing Andersen's impression of him as older and very worldly. As they were packing the bags, Daniel nonchalantly asked Andersen who the number one was at Rice. Although he already knew the answer, and had, in fact, researched the player, Andersen's answer gave him the information he was really looking for.

"Gary Richardson," Andersen said with a hint of disdain. Obviously there was no love lost between these two teammates. Daniel suspected as much, but needed the confirmation.

"Maybe I'll come a little early and watch him hit tomorrow," Daniel said.

"Suit yourself. Flash will put on a good show for you." Daniel could hear the disappointment in Andersen's reply, obviously thinking Daniel would dump him and opt for hitting with Gary instead, as soon as he saw his game.

"Oh, I just remembered I have an appointment right before this, so I may be a few minutes late." This wasn't really a lie on Daniel's part since he had rearranged his schedule to work with Jonathan right after school and still make it to tennis by six. This answer seemed to mollify Andersen some, and he hoped he would get at least one more practice with Daniel.

"What was that you called him? 'Flash'? Is that his nickname?" Daniel asked.

"Oh, hell no," Andersen quickly responded. "That's just what I call him when he's not around. Sorry. Please don't let on I call him that, Daniel. Coach McKenzie will crucify me if I do anything to upset Gary. And Gary hates the name. Besides, Gary's special. He's the coach's ticket to stardom when he goes pro. I doubt he'll finish Rice, but it's obvious Coach wants to be there when he does get on the tour."

"Your secret's safe with me," Daniel said as Andersen threw his bag on his back and took off for the field house. Daniel watched him run off as he was putting away his camera equipment. *There but for the grace of God go I,* he thought, remembering his father's fatalistic but humble quoting of John Bradford. *I reckon I'm growing up some since that old quote is speaking to me now.* But he knew exactly what he meant.

Andersen was a massive underachiever. He was obviously talented but had never had the quality coaching or guidance Daniel had always taken for granted. Daniel's research showed that Andersen had easily won his high school matches, and that got him to Rice, but his college career was less than exemplary, with a fifty percent win rate. From what Daniel had seen today, Andersen overcame poor mechanics with natural talent, and because his high school career was so successful, no one considered developing him. And here at Rice, being in the shadow of Gary and not having a demonstrative personality, he was ignored. Coach McKenzie was pouring all his effort into Gary, so Andersen coasted through assuming he was as good as he would ever be, and not being a winner, he wasn't worth extra effort.

How different Daniel's own career had been. He realized he had not had good coaches; he'd had great coaches, and all due to his father's behind-the-scenes manipulations. He had wanted to go to Florida Institute of Technology so he could surf at Melbourne Beach, but he was offered a scholarship at the University of Florida—a full ride if he maintained a B average. Little did he know at the time his father had orchestrated the scholarship and funded it. The coach there was phenomenal, and Daniel's tennis game grew remarkably under his tutelage.

When Daniel decided to go out west, applying to USC and UCLA for his master's, his father had said, "Those are great schools, but maybe you should check out Stanford while you're in Cali." So Daniel came up with the idea of going to Stanford—but not because of the school's reputation. Joseph wanted his son to attend Stanford so that he would play for Frank Hornbrook, a phenomenal coach who could prepare Daniel for a professional career.

Daniel was a very skillful player, but there was one aspect of his game his father wasn't able to corral. He had inherited his mother's emotional makeup along with her tall, svelte physique, wavy blond hair, and stunning looks. He didn't have the mental strength for the level of competition he would come to experience. He was a brooder, displaying a melancholy that caused him to recess into a safe haven of solitude where he could fight the demon of futility. His father had tried, and had been successful on many levels, to strengthen Daniel's mental game. But in the end, Daniel's emotions failed him. Joseph hoped Coach Hornbrook would toughen his son.

Daniel watched Andersen disappear around the building. He thought about him—average intelligence, normal emotions, satisfied with what life has dealt to him, happy just to be playing tennis. *He would blossom if given a little attention,* Daniel thought. He remembered his father had always gravitated toward the players and coaches like Andersen, and shied away from the Garys and McKenzies of the world—the glory-seekers and the showmen. He always looked for depth beneath the glossy exterior that fans worshipped.

Now, sitting on this bench with the sun fading in the west, Daniel felt his own failure. He wanted to apologize to his father now, to run to him and tell him all of his effort was not wasted. Daniel would find the strength his father thought wasn't there. He would do something his father would be proud of. What Daniel did not know—and would not for years to come—was that being Joseph's son was all Daniel ever had to do to win his father's pride. That was the depth and breadth of life, complete unto itself. But Daniel would have to become a father to learn how a father's love transcends all else in a son's life.

CHAPTER 18

coaching andersen

The next day, Andersen was waiting for Daniel when he got to the court at Galveston Racquet Club. Daniel could tell Andersen was eager to talk about something, but Daniel's time was precious now and he wanted to get started. He decided to give Andersen some leeway while he changed clothes and put on his shoes.

"How's it going, Andersen?" Daniel said as he sat on a bench and started changing his shoes.

"I was afraid you might not make it today."

"Would that matter?" Daniel coerced.

"Well, yesterday was the best workout I've had since I've been here," Andersen rushed on, "and obviously you are no weekend player, and the drills we ran were way better than what Coach McKenzie runs, so I know you know your stuff, so I was just hoping we'd be able to do it again and maybe you could help me some."

"Help you with what?" Daniel goaded.

"You know. Give me some pointers, help me with some of my shots, you know."

Daniel was enjoying watching Andersen beg, but he gave in slightly just to see if he could pull Andersen along. "I thought that was your coach's job. Doesn't he help you?"

"I told you, he's all wrapped up in Gary. He doesn't give a crap about me, and what he does tell me is shit I already know anyway."

Daniel could sense Andersen's frustration at Rice. That was a good sign. Andersen had gotten a glimpse yesterday that there was more available than what Coach McKenzie was offering, and it had lit a spark in him. *Yes,* Daniel thought, *that is very good. I might be able to work with this guy.*

"Tell you what I will do," Daniel said, as if he was going to concede a great treasure to Andersen. "I'll watch you while we drill today, and after practice, let's meet and talk about your game. Does Lloyd let you out at eight?"

Daniel had watched Andersen carefully yesterday, assessing his game without him realizing it. Some of the drills had actually been for Andersen's benefit so Daniel could gauge his shots. So even as he toyed with Andersen, the decision to help him had been a foregone conclusion in Daniel's mind.

"Yes, sir," Andersen said, hopefully.

Daniel heard the *sir* and knew his gambit had struck oil. He smiled inwardly. "Okay then, meet me at Rizzotto's at eight-fifteen and don't change clothes. Now, let's hit some balls."

Daniel stood and unzipped his racquet case, then paused and called out to Andersen. "By the way, Andersen, bring a DVD of Gary's matches." Andersen shrugged and walked onto the court.

After the practice session, Daniel watched Andersen until he was out of sight and then called Phillip Rogers. Phillip answered as Daniel was getting into his car.

"Hello?" Phillip said with his familiar sing-songy twang.

"Hi, Phillip. This is Daniel Furman."

"Trip, my boy, how's the hitting going? Is Andersen a backboard, or what?"

"It's going great, Phillip. He's exactly as you described. Thanks."

"Great, that's great. What can I do for you?"

"I noticed you still have the hard courts over in the woods. Are they in decent shape?" Daniel asked.

"Oh, yes," Phillip assured Daniel, who already knew they would be—Phillip took immense pride in the condition of his courts.

"Do they get used very much?"

"No, not really," Phillip confessed. "I have one doubles group that goes over there once a week, but they stay empty most of the time. It's a shame, too."

"I've got a crazy favor to ask," Daniel said.

"Shoot."

"Can I varnish one of the courts?"

"Varnish the court, huh?" Phillip mused, "The old Florida trick."

"I promise I'll clean it in a month and resurface it." Daniel knew this would be expensive, but he had heard the curiosity in Phillip's response and was hoping it may not be necessary.

"Use court number three. George power-washed it yesterday, so it should still be clean enough for the varnish. And don't worry about resurfacing. I may leave it as a varnished court. Some players love the speed, so it may just be a hit. I should have thought of that a long time ago, who knows?"

"Thanks," Daniel said. "One more question, then I promise I'll leave you alone."

"Yes?"

"What do you think of Lloyd McKenzie as a coach?"

"Ouch, Daniel." Daniel noticed the shift in the name and hoped he hadn't pushed Phillip too far.

"You know Rice pays me very well for the use of these facilities, so I'm not really keen on talking about their staff."

Daniel knew Phillip was on guard and didn't want to bite the hand that fed him, but he also felt Phillip was dying to tell someone his opinion of McKenzie.

"Phillip," Daniel said in as assuring a voice as he could muster, "whatever you tell me I will keep very private. Just between you and me. I would like to help Andersen with his game, and some knowledge of his coach might be helpful."

"Well, this better stay just between us."

"It will. I promise," Daniel said.

"He's a glory-seeker," Phillip began. "He likes the title of head coach much more than actually being a head coach, and his politics are impeccable. He says all the right things to all the right people, but in the end, he's just shined shit. He asked your father for a recommendation, and Joseph declined. I wish the president had listened to your dad, but Lloyd had schmoozed enough of the deans to overcome your dad's opinion. Rice has some great coaches, but he is not one of them."

"Wow. Tell me how you really feel," Daniel quipped.

Phillip laughed. "Okay, but you make sure you keep it to yourself."

"I will. Thanks. I've been getting the same feeling about him but needed some confirmation. I'm going to work with Andersen some on his game. You think Lloyd will be pissed?"

"Keep it quiet and low-key. Lloyd is so wrapped up in Gary right now he probably won't care. Just be careful."

"Good advice. I appreciate it. Talk to you later."

"One other thing, Daniel."

"Yeah?"

"I don't think Lloyd knows who you are. Apparently, your name change and cutting off all that curly blond hair has been successful. You better keep it that way, or Lloyd may take Andersen away just to spite your dad."

"Thanks. I'll stay very low-key," Daniel promised.

"Oh, and by the way, I think you have a fan. Some guy has been watching you and Andersen practice."

"Really? Who?" Daniel asked.

"I don't know. Never seen him before. I figured he might be a sponsor who's hoping you're about to get back in the game, and he wants to be the first to sign you."

"I guess I'll be disappointing him. Too bad. I was hoping nobody knew where I was. Oh, well. See you tomorrow."

Daniel headed to the hardware store. He had just enough time to get the varnish and rollers and then get to Rizzotto's to meet Andersen. Daniel picked up his laptop and headed into the restaurant. Andersen was waiting.

"Do you have the DVD?" Daniel asked, pulling the laptop out.

"Why do you want this DVD? You know I will be in deep shit if Coach McKenzie knows I took this out of the locker room," Andersen said with a worried look.

"Then be careful. Don't worry; it's nothing underhanded, and I'm not spying. I want you to look at Gary's game with me and find his Achilles' heel."

Daniel downloaded the DVD and handed it back to Andersen.

"Andersen," Daniel began, "I'll help you with your game if you won't get upset when I'm brutally frank with you. I don't have time to tell you how good your game is. All I have time for is to tell you where and how you need to improve, which means I will be criticizing you incessantly. And you have to be able to maintain a positive attitude, even though I'm tearing you apart. Can you handle that?"

"Can you help my game?"

"If you listen, learn, and work, yes. But it will get worse before it gets better."

"Why didn't you ask me for Dennis' DVD?" Dennis Boyer was Rice's number two player.

"Are you going to ask questions all night, or listen?"

"I'll listen," Andersen conceded, "but it still puzzles me that if I can't beat Dennis, then what chance do I have against Gary? Why not focus on Dennis?"

"It's a fair question. Do you think Dennis can beat Gary?" Daniel quizzed.

"Well, he hasn't yet, or he would be in the number one position; so obviously, no."

"I disagree," Daniel said. "I don't think Dennis wants to beat Gary. I think he likes the number two slot because it keeps him out from under McKenzie's thumb, he wins matches easier, and he still has the same scholarship. I think you will have an easier time against Gary than Dennis."

"Wait a minute. You think I can beat Gary?" Andersen's tone was rife with surprise.

"Don't you?"

"No, of course not!"

"That's your first big problem."

Daniel had manipulated the questions to get Andersen to this point. And here, Daniel could begin the tearing down in order to rebuild Andersen's game.

"You're a massive underachiever."

"WHAT?"

"That's not a positive attitude," Daniel reminded. "Don't get pissed or we end now."

"Okay. Sorry," Andersen said.

"Obviously you've never been criticized. You've cruised through an easy high school career and landed here purely on raw talent, and you've had the unfortunate fate of never having a coach who could or would assess your game to improve it. As long as you were winning, no one seemed to want to bother you. And anyone you lose to, you figure you can't beat, so you don't try."

Andersen was quiet and sullen, and Daniel wondered if he was pushing too far, too fast. But if he was going to pull this diamond out of the rough, he was going to have to generate some friction.

Daniel continued. "You've never learned how to assess the other player, to find his weaknesses and adjust your game to set up points to take advantage of those weaknesses. You have one game—hit it back one more time than your opponent and win by your opponent losing the point. That works against most of your competition at this level, but you are much better than that. You just don't know it and have never been pushed. And your game will not work against the top players. They manipulate your returns to set up a kill shot, and you don't even know it. So, together, we are going to learn when you are being set up and how to construct your own points to hit winners, not just returners."

Andersen was finally beginning to listen intently, seeing Daniel's criticisms did have a constructive end. And Daniel was right; no one had ever really given him any meaningful criticism. He just played his game and won, most of the time. But now, he was with someone who wasn't satisfied with "most of the time." Now Andersen was very uncomfortable, an emotion he was not familiar with at all. This was going far differently than he had imagined. He hoped he could hang with Daniel and felt like he had finally met someone he really did not want to disappoint.

Daniel continued the assessment. "You have about six decent shots, and each of those have mechanical errors in them keeping you from reaching your full potential. You need to be proficient with at least thirty shots and know when to use them and how to set them up. Fortunately for you, you are immensely talented, so you will be able to learn the shots quickly. Getting proficient will be the hardest and will require the most work. You will have to do that on your own, with a camera, so you don't drop back into old habits. I can review the videos and help, but I just don't have time otherwise. Your footwork is horrible, but you have lightning-fast reflexes, on par with race-car drivers and champion ping-pong players. That has allowed you to overcome the poor footwork. We can substantially improve that.

"In tennis, at the professional level, thousandths of a second make huge differences. You are a tenth of a second behind, which is an eternity. Your quickness has allowed you to react to shots instead of anticipating shots and being ahead of them. To anticipate shots, you have to learn how to assess your opponent's game quickly and learn to see ahead, much like a chess master sees many moves ahead. You'll learn how to see several shots ahead instantly, knowing the scenario will probably change with each shot. But you will be prepared. Oh, and your serve is horrible."

"I thought I had a pretty decent serve!" Andersen said defensively.

"Really?" Daniel countered. "Well, quit thinking and listen. Your feet start in the wrong position; your toss starts too high, and it is not consistent enough or controlled enough; your grip is wrong; your racquet starts too low; you pause your swing midway; you don't bring your racquet low enough down your back; you don't break your wrist when you strike the ball; your spin is measly and always the same; and your follow-through is down your right side instead of crossing over and allowing your right foot to start your approach, following your serve to the net. And that's just for starters. Any questions? That's rhetorical, don't answer. When we start working on your serve, I'll show you many more things wrong, including how you telegraph to your opponent if you are hitting to his forehand or backhand. Get it?"

"Yes, sir," Andersen said quietly. "Did you see all that today?"

"I began assessing your game the moment you shook my hand," Daniel said. "And I researched your game before I walked on the court. I have you on video. When I moved the camera out of the way and you thought I was finished filming, it was actually still on and pointed at you. I know more about your game than you do. I know more about Dennis' game than you do, and I know more about Gary's game than you. And that's pitiful on your part. You are going to learn to do your homework so that when you step onto a court, you are fully prepared to pick apart your opponent, both physically and mentally."

"Wow. I've never thought that much about tennis," Andersen said. "I never even knew to think that much about tennis, and I never knew there was homework involved in tennis. I just played."

"Well, that's going to change if you want to get to the upper level of competition," Daniel said.

"You think I can do that?"

"Like I said at the beginning, you're a massive underachiever. So we are going to let you achieve your potential. My father always told me the only thing he could not teach was talent. It had to be there or all the coaching and training and drilling was for naught. But talent isn't enough, and training isn't enough. You have to have a burning desire to excel. You have to live, breathe, eat, and sleep tennis to get to the level of competition you are capable of. Are you willing to do that?"

"Yes, I think so," Andersen said.

"That's not good enough. Sorry. Let's just forget it," Daniel said as he closed his laptop.

"No, Daniel! I can. I will. I promise!" Andersen said, willing Daniel not to leave.

"That's better. Let's go varnish a court."

"What?"

"Just come on. You'll see," Daniel said.

• • •

For the next week, Daniel worked with Andersen, tearing his game away and infusing a powerful, new, multifaceted game into his core. The varnished court provided a speed Andersen had never experienced, but what he found was as his senses adjusted to the fast pace of the varnish, the other courts became easier and easier to time and react to. Daniel gave Andersen's footwork a makeover that not only shortened his time to the ball, but also set him up perfectly for the shot, improving accuracy, power, and ball movement, all with just footwork. Andersen had never realized when turning to a forehand, he first moved his right foot back and then his left foot across, costing him precious time, position, and power. The same was true of his backhand, only in reverse. Daniel showed him the classic cross-over move, the same one baseball infielders use to get to balls quickly and efficiently. Everything Daniel taught built on the previous mechanics, so Andersen's game was reborn from the foundation. All the drills were designed as part of the building process, so each piece of the puzzle was reinforced and strengthened.

Daniel was amazed how quickly Andersen picked up new strokes, new moves, and new techniques, and mastered them. Daniel's hunch was verified; Andersen was immensely talented and had the ability to be a top player. Daniel could only hope it wasn't too late and that Andersen's poor mechanics would not resurface under pressure.

Andersen became a workhorse. He would be on the court at five each morning and drill with the machine before his eight o'clock classes. He did not wait until the team showed up at four for the afternoon practice; he was there at two, and he spent his spare moments anywhere doing his schoolwork—all this to be ready for Daniel to show up at six and take him through a new lesson and new drills. Daniel would give him a set of priorities to work on when he wasn't there and would review his mechanics, meticulously critiquing each aspect of Andersen's strokes. Daniel also gave Andersen a set of stretches to do before starting any workout, explaining how important each stretch was to the particular muscles or group of muscles. Andersen was learning the totality of higher-level tennis, and for the first time in his life, he was excited about the game. He was still surprised about how far off his service mechanics had been, since his serve had always been mildly successful due to his ability to muscle it over with enough pace to give weaker players trouble.

"A proper service motion," Daniel had told him the day they started to rebuild this part of his game, "is like a very complicated dance step. It has rhythm and grace, with a fluidity that builds toward the final striking of the ball, and smooth follow-through transitioning to the next shot. Everything about it garners power and control as well as disguises the shot until the ultimate moment of impact. A heavy topspin is the hardest to disguise because the toss needs to be at the eleven o'clock position and the racquet needs to come over the top, similar to a curve ball from a pitcher. It's hard to disguise, but so effective. Learn to change its pace slightly, which you *can* disguise, and it becomes a formidable weapon."

Daniel spent two hours taking Andersen through the serve routine, and Andersen missed Coach McKenzie's films. As he told Daniel the next day, "The punishment was well worth the time with you."

"Well, we'll have to be a lot more careful about that. I don't want any eyebrows raised about our time together until you are ready. Be sure, when you're practicing with your team, you give no hints of what we're doing. Also, don't drop back into old habits. I know that sounds contradictory, but you can figure it out. And remember, one of the most powerful psychological weapons in your arsenal is to have your opponent underestimate you. Give nothing away. When you go up against Gary, I want him to think it's just another easy win."

"So, you think I can beat Gary?" Andersen said hopefully.

"No. Not yet," Daniel said. "But eventually. Otherwise, I doubt I would be spending so much time and resources with you. And, when you are ready, you will not be asking that question. You will be telling me how, when, and where you are going to beat him and take over the number one spot. After that, you will probably leave Rice. But that's way off yet. Let's get to work."

Andersen opened the new balls, looked at the sun, and took a court side. *He's learning quickly and naturally,* Daniel thought.

CHAPTER 19

eric attacks

"**D**aniel?"

"Yes, Jennifer?"

"Victor wants to see you in his office, immediately."

"Sounds ominous. What's up?" Daniel said as the studio's intercom crackled.

"No idea, but Eric isn't in his office. Don't know if it means anything, though."

"Thanks. Would you let Sarah know I'm on my way?" Daniel asked.

"Already did. And the elevator is on the way."

"I'll catch the stairs. Thanks."

Daniel had gotten up out of his new chair, where he had been reading reports while drinking his morning mug of green tea with a spoonful of the brown sugar Victor had introduced to him. It was his only concession to sugar, which he avoided otherwise. He took a quick look around his office, wondering if he should take anything and decided not to, since he didn't know what the sudden meeting was about. His gaze paused at the chair. He was still amazed at the architect's transformation. Daniel had told him the redesign far exceeded his expectations. Then the architect made a request that at first seemed odd, but after Daniel thought about it, made perfect sense. He said to live in it for a couple of weeks, let it grow on him, and note anything that may not be working out perfectly for him. A week later, he dropped in to see Daniel and talk to him about the office. By then Daniel did have some comments. Daniel told him he reads a lot of technical reports, sometimes for an extended period of time, and the stools at the table are not conducive to that. He knew he had said he had an aversion to chairs, especially ones with high backs, but asked if he could compromise the design and bring in one chair. The architect immediately said no. "We don't compromise the design." Then he smiled and said, "We reach a consensus in the design. In a compromise, everyone loses something; in a consensus, everyone's a winner. I've already selected your chair. I thought you would eventually want one, but it has to be one that speaks to your space and to those who visit you. You see, furniture has a language like people have a body language. Sometimes it can scream at you."

"Sort of like Eric's?" Daniel pondered. The architect smiled a small, sardonic smile and nodded with a little shrug. Obviously, he was not into criticizing a colleague's designs, but it was equally clear Daniel had hit home with the question.

"Your chair, Daniel," he continued, "must say to your guests *I am Daniel's* without saying *I am the most important thing in this room.*"

"How will it do that?" Daniel quizzed.

"With its size, leather color and texture, arms, small low bookshelf as its companion, and most importantly, its position in the room. We will also give it its own Tizio lamp, so there are three items making a group."

"Why three?"

"Well, two evokes tension by competition for top dog, while three creates a community. I know these are small nuances, but they're the unspoken gestures of design creating the sense of place. Visitors may know the space has proper feel—a balance—but will not know exactly why. Like a musical composition with all the notes in place. It just feels right."

Daniel's thoughts went to Mishael and her music, and he knew when he sat in this chair, he would think of her.

His furniture arrived and was placed exactly as the architect had specified. Daniel noticed two things in very short order. When visitors came into his office, they made no attempt to sit in the chair; they pulled up a stool and sat at the table. The chair quietly said, *I am Daniel's*. The other was how serenely comfortable it was for reading his reports. At first he thought it was too small, but he quickly learned it was just right. When the architect called to enquire about it, Daniel asked him why the bookshelf was so small. "What happens if I get too many books for it?"

"Well," the architect said, "then you will have too many books, so get rid of some. Stay light. Maybe you can put them on Eric's bookshelf and make sure they are never touched again."

Daniel laughed. Now he knew his architect did have a sense of humor, albeit very dry.

Daniel took the stairs two at a time, paused, and took a deep breath before opening the door to Sarah's office and calmly walking in. Sarah nodded toward Victor's double doors, indicating to go in, so Daniel grasped the brass door handles and, feeling the smoothness of the expensive hardware, pushed open the heavy wooden doors.

Victor's office was very large, in a corner of the building with windows covering two walls. He had a large sitting area with a gas fireplace where Daniel had had his first meeting, a full-size conference table in another area, and his desk with two guest chairs finishing out the main space. Daniel saw a doorway in a richly paneled wall he guessed led to Victor's private area. He had heard Victor had complete living quarters there with a gourmet-fitted kitchen, as well as a bath with whirlpool, sauna and steam room, closet with a complete wardrobe, one large bedroom, and a second small one for his French domestic valet, Robert, who would stay there if Victor had a late evening. Hearing Victor roll his *r* when he pronounced *Ro'bear* amused Daniel, but he never let it show.

Daniel noticed Eric in one of the guest chairs, so he walked over to sit in the other chair as he nodded an acknowledgment to Eric. Eric ignored him. *So, he's declared war,* Daniel thought. *Or maybe he's already launched a lethal salvo, and I'm dead and don't know it yet.*

Daniel knew how hard it was to get an audience with Victor, so certainly Eric had a massive arsenal arrayed against him or Victor would not have given him the time of day. Possibly this was Eric's version of Pearl Harbor, the surprise Japanese attack that had nearly destroyed America's Pacific fleet and thrust the United States into World War II.

Daniel loved history, and his father had always encouraged him to take as many liberal arts courses as his engineering schedule would allow. "Engineering is stale and lifeless without the humanities," his father had told him. "Humanities are where you acquire the wisdom to apply the technical knowledge you will gain." Daniel had taken extra courses beyond his elective fulfillment; anthropology, sociology, psychology, and as much history as time allowed.

Now, Daniel wondered if it was a lethal surprise attack. Had Eric awakened a sleeping giant, as Admiral Yamamoto had so aptly concluded after the Pearl Harbor attack, or was Daniel's career at VCM sunk? Daniel felt panic building deep within and his knees were beginning to feel numb.

Daniel felt a tingling in his shoulder and then he remembered his trip to Lake Ellen when he was about six years old. Growing up in Florida, his mom and dad would take him to Lake Ellen to play in the water on hot summer days. Lake Ellen is one of the myriad of beautiful spring-fed lakes gracing central Florida. It is protected from alligator intrusions and checked daily by the lifeguards. It has a dock with a diving board, a slide and other water play equipment, and several floating docks for kids to push out into the water and play from. On one trip, Daniel was playing on one of the docks near the shoreline when a group of older boys decided to push it out to deep water while he was still on it. Daniel watched as the boys repeatedly jumped off the dock and climbed back up the ladder. He decided he could do it, so he jumped in and splashed his way back to the ladder. After doing this several times, he noticed his dad watching from the shore. His dad motioned for him to stay on the dock and then came out to join him. "Where did you learn to swim, Trip?" his dad asked as he climbed the ladder.

"Right here. I watched those boys and did what they did." His dad didn't tell him until he was much older how scared he was when he saw Daniel out on the dock, knowing he could not swim. He said he couldn't get to him fast enough, but at the time, Daniel thought nothing of it; he was just having fun like the older boys. His father asked him if he could swim to the slide. Daniel looked at it and jumped in and started splashing toward it, his father watching intently. Suddenly Daniel looked up and saw the slide was still far away and the dock was far away and he couldn't make it. He panicked. He started screaming and kicking and splashing to keep his head above the water's surface. Through the splashing he saw his father dive into the water, barely making a ripple, and swim with several strong, smooth strokes to Daniel. Daniel felt his father's strong hand under the small of his back and heard his father tell him to stand up. "I can't, I can't!" Daniel yelled in full panic mode. "TRIP!" his father barked, "STAND UP!" Daniel forced his feet down, knowing the water was over his head. Immediately his toes touched the sandy bottom and he stood up; the water was barely to his chest. His father was on his knees beside him, just looking at him. Daniel felt acute embarrassment under his father's stare and looked around. Nobody seemed to have noticed his foray into a near-death experience. "Now, Trip," his father said patiently, "let's learn to swim properly." His father showed him first how to cup his hands and fingers together so they would act as paddles, and how to move them through the water efficiently while kicking in rhythm and breathing from beneath his armpit.

His father taught him to swim that day, but the lesson Daniel really learned was how silly panic was. Countless times afterward, when Daniel would feel his anxiety rising, he would see his father swimming toward him and remember the panic was probably far more detrimental than the situation invoking it. He thought of his father swimming toward him now, and his panic subsided.

Daniel ignored Eric's stoicism as he turned his attention toward Victor. He smelled the rich, firm leather and noticed the straighter-than-normal back and arm rests, just slightly too narrow for comfort. He smiled to himself briefly, listening to what the chair was saying. *You are here for a very good reason. Do not get comfortable. Pay attention.* Daniel remembered his architect was also Victor's, or vice versa, and his appreciation grew another notch as he heard the chair, something he never imagined could communicate, and knew the architect had selected these chairs and placed them perfectly to elicit exactly that feeling, whether the user recognized it or not.

"Daniel," Victor began with a grave tone as he looked over the top of his reading glasses. "Eric has made some serious allegations about how you obtained the Hudson building and Trans-Gulf contracts. He says you stole them from him. Can you explain how you came by them?"

Daniel paused and willed himself to stay off the defensive. He remembered what he had told Jonathan at the batting cage about always being truthful, and gathered his thoughts to ensure he did so. He wondered again if this was to be his Pearl Harbor: Had Eric's surprise conference with Victor been his way to destroy Daniel with an unprovoked attack? He felt the weight of the dawning war, and took a deep breath as if marshaling his forces, and began. "Well, Henry Hudson called me and—"

"That's a lie!" Eric interrupted. "He called Henry Hudson. On Henry's private line only I have!"

Before Daniel could respond, Victor broke in. "Eric, you will keep quiet while Daniel is talking. If you can't, I'll send you out and hear Daniel privately."

"But Victor—" Eric started. Victor put his hand up and motioned to the door.

"I'll keep quiet," Eric relented.

"That's your last warning. Well, Daniel?"

Daniel picked up his conversation, his tone unchanged by the caustic volley. His insides were churning, doubting, trying to find where he had violated any of VCM's strict protocols about interoffice dealings.

"Technically," he said coolly, "Eric is correct." He saw the impish smile start to form on Eric's face. "I did call Mr. Hudson. I was returning *his* call."

"On his—" Eric interrupted, stopping when Victor impatiently glared at him. Daniel finished the sentence.

"Yes. On his private line. He called from his car, and Jennifer told him I was away from my desk for a moment. I was in the toilet. Henry asked Jen to have me call him back in his office in fifteen minutes and gave her the number. If Eric will look through the phone log again, he will see a private name, private caller incoming fifteen minutes before my outgoing call. That will be Mr. Hudson's car phone, which I believe only you, Victor, have the number for."

He glanced toward Eric as he said this. The implication that Eric did not have Henry Hudson's car phone number was a barb in his underbelly, and his reaction indicated he did not even know about the phone, let alone receiving a phone call from it.

It was a small victory for Daniel and stemmed the obvious momentum Eric had assumed was his. Daniel quickly made a promise to himself to stay off the attack as well as the defensive, and maintain a high road by simply stating facts.

"And what did Henry want?" Victor asked. It was clear from his familiar tone that Victor and Henry knew each other beyond just being peers in the business world of Houston. Daniel saw the subtle slump of Eric's shoulders.

So, Daniel thought, *Eric doesn't know what close friends Victor and Henry are.* He packaged that information away to be savored for a future exchange, if needed.

"Well, the first call was to set up a meeting at his building, which I agreed to, and I asked that Jennifer and his secretary set the time and date convenient for him. I slipped a note to Jen asking her to make it several days out so I would have time to do my homework on Mr. Hudson."

Victor, although listening intently, asked, "You didn't make the meeting as quickly as possible, knowing the potential value?" He was looking at Eric as he asked the question. Obviously, the answer would affect Eric, but Daniel couldn't figure out how or why, so again, he stayed the course of blind honesty.

"I absolutely knew its potential value, Victor, which is why I wanted to be as prepared as possible when I did meet Mr. Hudson. Jennifer bought me two days, which I used every minute of to find out all I could about him—his company, his holdings, and especially his beloved building."

Victor, still looking at Eric, asked, "Have you ever spent two days learning about Henry Hudson, Eric?"

"Well, I thought—" Eric started, but was cut off by Victor's sudden strike.

"Don't bullshit me, Eric! That's a yes or no question, and I don't have time for your inane excuses."

Obviously, without Eric saying so, the answer was no, which was exactly where Victor had wanted to go with his question. Suddenly, and to Eric's complete surprise, all of his imagined momentum vanished. Daniel had not anticipated this at all, and was almost too stupefied to continue. Victor prodded him.

"And what did your research tell you, Daniel?" Victor's voice was now like that of a father talking to his son after putting down a neighborhood bully who had been harassing him. Daniel continued in the same monotonous, factual voice, not wanting to show any indication of elation or confidence, something Eric would have worn on his shirt sleeve.

"Besides being a self-made millionaire coming from a tenant farmer's family, he holds real estate in and around Houston that is varied and unique. He seems to have a rather eclectic sense of taste in what he owns, and he takes immense pride in each of his properties. But his building downtown, which is his pride and joy and should be the jewel of his holdings, is rather like his prodigal son. It is very unprofitable, and even if he could get his leases to a hundred percent, he can't command enough income to offset his overhead. It appears to be a sinking ship, and due to new energy requirements and ADA issues, he is very wary to start any renovations, afraid he will have to demolish half the building to bring it up to code."

"What did you do?" Victor asked, calmly.

"I called our architect." Daniel saw Eric twitch as he used the term "our" and almost caught a tiny grin from Victor. He continued without missing a beat, as if the term had been used thousands of times. "Our architect met with me at the building and gave me a great number of ideas and strategies for the building. He told me about a new building code Texas has adopted called the International Existing Building Code, or IEBC, that has been written to address America's many aging buildings, their owners fearing they have little recourse but to tear them down. The IEBC allows owners and architects to renovate portions of the aging building while allowing portions to remain as they are, even though not up to current code. It also recognizes that many buildings may be sub-standard, but have been used successfully for many years, and so accepts them as they are without penalty. The architect also went over the accessibility issues, and he talked about technical infeasibility. Basically, if a structure will not allow a hundred percent compliance with the Americans with Disabilities Act, then the designer can upgrade as much as possible short of making major structural changes, and the building official must accept that. Another interesting caveat is that Mr. Hudson doesn't have to spend more than twenty percent of his budget upgrading to current accessible standards. It was great information to give to Mr. Hudson."

Victor nodded as if giving Daniel a pat on the back, and Eric sank a little lower into his chair.

"Then we talked about the enormous energy bills Mr. Hudson pays for the building. The architect asked about repair and maintenance bills that have been paid over the past five years. I had them with me in my file, thanks to Jennifer; she was unbelievably helpful." This compliment of Jennifer in Victor's presence was really meant as a slap in the face to Eric for his treatment of her. Victor's nod signaled the rebuke had hit its mark.

"The architect immediately called his mechanical engineer, who met us on the roof of the building where the antiquated HVAC units were. While the architect was examining the roof, the engineer was assessing the units. The architect concluded the old built-up roofing system was way past its life span, so continued patching of it was a waste of money. The engineer had similar things to say about the units. Basically, they should have been replaced years ago. We also discovered the roofing contractor who has been repairing the roof is related to the mechanical contractor who has been fixing the units, so obviously they thought they had found a cash cow, a source of continual, easy income, and so were bilking Mr. Hudson.

"I put together an entire maintenance and replacement schedule, showing costs and savings, including a new white membrane roof for solar reflectivity, and new polyisocyanurate insulation. The old roof had none at all. With that and new windows—the architect recommended a window manufacturer that specializes in historic-looking windows with through-the-pane mullions and wide casings, but modern double glazing for excellent thermal properties—the mechanical engineer ran an energy analysis for me and showed how the energy savings would pay for the upgrades and new mechanical system in five years or less. Then the architect talked to us about historic tax credits, both state and federal, as well as inexpensive money from the power company for energy-related upgrades, and with all that, it was a no-brainer to start renovating the building."

"Assuming you could lease space in it," Victor chimed in.

"I was getting to that," Daniel continued. Eric had leaned forward by now, head in his hands, like a whipped puppy. "Our architect found the building's construction plans in the city archives and discovered it originally had a beautiful three-story atrium that's now floored over to make more rentable area, but which had left the entrance and lobby area woefully dismal and cavern-like. He suggested opening it back up and restoring the atrium to its original grandeur. Mr. Hudson balked at this, but the architect explained that not only would the entire building be more desirable, and hence more rentable, but the offices overlooking the atrium would bring a premium, offsetting the loss of leasable square footage. Then he put the nail in the coffin by stating they are unrentable now anyway, so what does it hurt if that area goes away? Mr. Hudson couldn't argue, so the architect was given the green light to design the renovations. Which leads me to the marketing.

"I know we have an excellent marketing department here, Victor, but their program is just not up to what Mr. Hudson needs for a historic building. I found a firm in Atlanta specializing in marketing historic properties, and they have a list of tenants who look for these types of spaces to occupy because they match the image the companies want to convey. The Atlanta group put together a marvelous presentation for Mr. Hudson, so he went with them. Sorry, but I thought it was critical to the success of the project."

Victor nodded his understanding and motioned Daniel to continue.

"Well, what about TGP?" Eric blurted, like a school-age child ratting out a rival. Victor didn't respond but sat back and let Daniel continue, unabated, into the Trans-Gulf Petroleum contracts.

"I believe Mr. Hudson was pleased with our work and mentioned it to Harry Lyalls, CEO of TGP, and his close friend." Eric looked over at Daniel, for the first time making brief eye contact. *So, he didn't know they were friends either,* Daniel thought. He stored that information in the same compartment as Victor and Henry's friendship, and continued into the TGP saga.

"As you know, Victor, I have a master's degree in civil engineering, with an emphasis on construction, as well as an MBA, so the petroleum industry is very easy for me to comprehend." Daniel knew Eric's pre-law degree from the University of Virginia did not give him the technical expertise to accommodate TGP's needs for their structures, so mentioning his own education was, by inference, another barb projected toward Eric. *The high road,* Daniel reminded himself, *stick to a high road.*

"Mr. Hudson gave me Harry Lyalls' number," Daniel made sure he got that information out quickly so Eric would not question where the number came from, "and asked me to call him the next week. He said Harry was out of the country until then, but he had spoken with him about me, so Harry was expecting my call. That gave me plenty of time to research TGP and figure out how VCM could service them. I'm working on a program that links their on-shore and off-shore facilities into a comprehensive schedule of upkeep, maintenance, and energy usage so their expenses are not only predictable, but apportioned evenly on a monthly basis, and when upgrades and replacements are due, there is funding for it already in place. Mr. Lyalls and I are meeting on a weekly basis to review progress and implement the program. I'm also reviewing the plans for his new facilities and expansions." Daniel paused.

"Is that all?" Victor asked.

"Unless you or Eric have any questions, or you want me to elaborate," Daniel answered.

"No," Victor said, before Eric could try to question or comment, "but I do want to add something."

Both Daniel and Eric were keenly attentive.

"I know our architect and his engineer are both LEED professionals and you have been studying to take the exam to become LEED-certified. By the way, Eric, LEED means Leadership in Energy and Environmental Design. It's a green building certification."

Eric winced.

"Yes, sir," Daniel politely acknowledged, "I'm scheduled to take it next week."

"I'm thinking about requiring all of our associates to be LEED-certified. What do you think?" Victor directed the question at Daniel alone.

"I don't think it's an option anymore in our business. I think it's a necessity in order to be able to manage the buildings we represent. More of them are either becoming LEED-certified or are built as a LEED building initially, but LEED is not a one-time certificate a building gets. It's an ongoing process, and if not maintained, a building can lose its certification, so it's imperative we know and understand those ramifications. Even the way floors are cleaned and trash is handled has LEED points assigned to it." Daniel wanted desperately to watch Eric's reaction, but he kept his focus squarely on Victor. Victor, however, was watching Eric and giving nothing away.

"Great, Daniel," Victor concluded, "my thoughts exactly, which is why I'm having Sarah prepare the memorandum that will go out this afternoon. I would like you to review it before it goes out. I've asked Sarah to have a copy waiting for you when you step out. I'd like a moment alone with Eric while you review it, and then I'd like you to come back in for a final item of business. Thank you, Daniel."

Daniel thanked Victor and got up for the long walk to the double doors. Victor started in on Eric before Daniel was on his feet. Obviously, he wanted Daniel to hear some of what he said, but not everything.

"Eric, apparently you have acted on some very dubious information."

"But Jennifer gave—"

At that instant, Victor saw Daniel pause in mid-stride and clench his fist. Victor could sense the hackles on Daniel's neck rise, but he did not stop walking. *Just the reaction I was hoping for,* thought Victor. *He is cool and calm when the attacks are directed at him, but a volcano ready to erupt if he senses an injustice.* The entire thought took only an instant, so it gave Victor ample time to cut Eric short and prevent Daniel's explosive response.

"Eric!" Victor snapped, the venom apparent, "Don't even think about passing the responsibility for your actions to anyone else, especially Jennifer!" Victor saw Daniel's fist relax and his stride continue, barely broken. Victor continued, "You assumed something from information without checking it for the truth, and jumped to damaging conclusions."

By this time Daniel had opened the door, and as it closed behind him the voices were cut to silence. Daniel noticed the solidity of the doors and the substantial seals around the edge. *Completely sound-proof,* he thought. Sarah was waiting for him with a memo. Daniel paused as he took it.

"Victor knew exactly how that meeting was going to turn out before I walked in there, didn't he?" Daniel asked.

"Why do you say that, Daniel?" Sarah was incredibly nonchalant with the question.

"Otherwise why would you be standing here with this memo, waiting on me?"

"I don't know. What do you think?" With that, Sarah had given away absolutely nothing, but in the same words told Daniel all he wanted to know. Daniel had just been perfectly played by Victor. This was his court, and his game, and he was the master of it. Daniel shrugged, his admiration for Victor growing. He was about to sit and read the memo, when Victor's door opened and Eric walked out, red-faced and fuming.

"I hope I see you Saturday!" Eric spit. "I'm going to enjoy wiping the court with you!" Daniel, outwardly calm, just replied, "I still have to make it past Billy and David to get to the finals. And you're not there yet, either."

"But I will be," Eric announced with bravado. "I just hope you can make it!"

"I reckon so," Daniel said as if it were nothing, giving no credence to Eric's threat. Eric slammed Sarah's door and was gone. Sarah looked over at Daniel and raised one eyebrow, then flashed a beautiful smile. Daniel finally allowed a smile to emerge from his game-face facade. It was a big smile. He had just sunk the third aircraft carrier, just like the United States did at Midway to the Japanese, turning the tide of the war in the Pacific. He then cautioned himself: after Midway there were three bloody years of war and thousands of lives lost before Truman brought the war to an abrupt halt at Hiroshima and Nagasaki. *Men are truly horrible creatures,* he thought. Then he remembered the rebuilding of Japan after the war. He thought about Japan and how they had become a great US ally throughout the Cold War years. *I wonder if Eric and I will ever reconcile like that.*

Sarah interrupted his thoughts. "Victor will see you now," she said and opened the door with her back, forcing Daniel to slip closely by her. Her perfume was a heavenly fragrance, and Daniel wanted to stop the world there for a moment. But Victor beckoned him and Sarah eased forward, closing the door behind her.

Victor had come around from behind his desk and taken one of the chairs. He motioned Daniel to the other one, still warm from his previous session. Victor had turned each chair slightly toward the other, creating a forum for an equal-to-equal dialogue. Daniel wondered if their architect had showed this to Victor, or maybe learned it from Victor. Either way, again, he heard the language of the furniture, as well as Victor's gesture to have a personal talk with him. Victor's intercom came to life. Although Daniel could not ascertain where the sound actually came from, it was perfectly clear with not a hint of a crackle. He saw Victor reach into his coat pocket, presumably to push a button on a remote. Daniel saw a red light on the desk turn green, and Victor answered Sarah's announcement that his next appointment had arrived and was waiting. He asked her to apologize for him and give him ten minutes. Daniel knew this was tantamount to sacrilege for Victor, and so was honored by the action.

"I can come back later," Daniel offered. But Victor refused by just pointing to the seat, directing Daniel to sit.

"Daniel," Victor began, "you've really done an outstanding job in the short time you've been here. I know your father would be proud. You do have one area we need to work on. You were blindsided today by Eric because you are so naive about politics. Office and business politics is more important than all of your technical expertise, because if you get torpedoed by it, you will never get to use all that knowledge. Consider today your first lesson. And as a clincher, remember this: politics is ninety percent perception and ten percent reality. Some people think the ten percent figure is high. You get it. It's a deadly game, and right now you're in everyone's crosshairs."

"Thanks, Victor," Daniel said, truly appreciating his extra time and caring enough to warn him. "I will have to figure out how to learn *politics*."

"Time and experience are really the only ways. But knowing what to look for is essential to making that experience pay off," Victor concluded.

"May I ask a question?" Daniel really wanted to get the most out of his session with Victor and wanted to ask a million questions, but would start with one.

"Sure," Victor said. "There's no guarantee of an answer though," he continued through a smile.

"Did you feed Jennifer information to give to Eric?"

"Wow! That's a perceptive question, Daniel. Sarah warned me about your political *un*-correctness. Let me answer this way: whatever information Eric got and how he got it is not nearly as important as how he interpreted it. Information unto itself is not really relevant until its contextual relationship to other information is determined. Otherwise, it is very dangerous. Eric took innocent information and warped it to fit his delusion, and when the information did not fit his desired purpose, he manipulated it until it did. Sarah told me you thought, early on, that Eric has a massive ego. Massive egos aren't necessarily bad. They can breed confidence. The problem is, they are most often confused with narcissism, which is extremely dangerous to be on the receiving end of. You should study it, preferably before Saturday." This last comment puzzled Daniel, so he stored it away to be figured out later.

"One last thing, Daniel." Victor reached over to his desk and retrieved a large envelope and handed it to Daniel. "This is the deed to your dad's and my cabin in Maine, as well as other relevant information. We owned most of the mountain and have kept it very inaccessible. A very close friend of mine, Susan Stratford, is the caretaker of it. She's a bit of a recluse, but I require her to check in with Sarah every week or we send the sheriff to check on her. I ask you continue that. The property is now yours, as you can see from the deed. We rent it out, very exclusively, to a select few, for about four weeks a year. That's enough income to pay all the expenses and give Susan enough for food and necessities. Let her know when you want to go there. She will have everything ready, and she will disappear when you arrive. Afterward, just walk away. She will take care of everything. It gives her something to do."

"Thank you, Victor. But why?" Daniel asked.

"Why give it to you, or why now?"

"I guess why me and why now?"

"It was always our intention that the survivor of the two of us would inherit the partner's share, so when your dad died, it all came to me. I always thought I would go well before your dad. My lifestyle and genes really aren't geared to longevity, so I assumed it would be yours anyway. And I don't care to go there anymore now that Joseph won't be there. We had fantastic vacations there and I just want to keep the memories. Why now? Why not now? There's no point in me holding on to it. And you've shown me you are responsible enough to handle it."

Daniel started to get up, but Victor placed a hand on his arm. "Oh, another thing, Daniel. If Susan dies there, please have her buried on the mountain. That's what she wants. Very few people even know she exists, and she likes it that way. I haven't seen her face in ten or fifteen years, so I don't even think I would recognize her, so let's keep it that way. She's also been doing some very sensitive research there that cannot fall into the public domain. Protect it for her. There's a contact's name in the folder for forwarding the research."

"Sure, Victor, no problem," Daniel said.

"Ten minutes, Victor." Daniel heard Sarah's voice and saw the light change on the desk, and Victor responded, "Thanks, Sarah. Send them in. Daniel is on his way out."

Daniel got up and shook Victor's hand. Victor's handshake was firm and sincere, and an instant longer than necessary, indicating the bond Victor felt with his best friend's son. *I wish there was a way I could entice him to stay,* Victor thought. But he knew Daniel's inner drum beat a different beat drowning out all others, and he would follow it, blindly, without regard to consequence. *So different a person than Eric,* Victor thought. He had learned a long time ago every organization has its Erics, and you can't beat them away with sticks. They infect you like a cancer, and the best you can do is deal with them. At least Victor had learned to deal with them; he could take some solace in that. He often wondered if that was why Joseph never became part of any large organization: he would not subject himself to the Erics. He had no tolerance for them. And the Daniels? They are the jewels to be appreciated while you have them, and let go gracefully, as a fleeting moment. Victor watched him walk away. He had his mother's walk, but he was definitely his father's son.

Daniel reflected on his encounter as he headed toward the double doors, passing Victor's next appointment with hardly an acknowledgment. He was lost in thought. The truth had saved him today. He felt that. And the same advice he had given young Jonathan their first day at the batting cage had paid dividends today. His father had given him the exact speech early in life, and he had just repeated it to Jonathan as part of the training. But today, he had lived his father's words, not just repeated them. He wanted to thank his father, to run to him and hug him and get picked up and thrown over his father's head again like when he was a child. *I miss you, Dad,* he thought.

CHAPTER 20

eric's bravado

C raig, the club pro, was studying the tournament scoreboard hanging on the wall of the Westmoreland Country Club Pro Shop as Eric came through the door and approached it. Craig moved away, slipping behind the clothes rack and back to his office, which had a large plate glass window looking onto the pro shop. Cheryl Taussig, a local high school player, was working the counter when Eric, after looking at all the scores, turned to her.

"What do you think of the tournament, Cheryl?" Eric asked as he leaned on the counter to get slightly closer to her, her shorts showing off her thighs. She rotated on the tall stool she was sitting partially on, revealing the bulge of her small breasts, and Eric leaned farther over the service counter for a better look.

None of this was lost on Craig. He had been watching Eric talk up Cheryl ever since she started working at the pro shop. Eric got his little ego boost by having a seventeen-year-old fawn on him, and she was thrilled by the attention of an older, wealthy man—*older* meaning anyone five years her senior, and *wealthy* meaning he drove an expensive car. Craig was hoping he would try something with her so he could get Eric ousted from the club and possibly press charges for molesting a minor, but Eric was all show and no action. So the show continued, with Cheryl using the stool as a prop for enticement and Eric barely concealing his lecherous looks.

"Oh, you're doing fantastic, Mr. Shoemaker," Cheryl responded, naively stroking his ego.

"Well, I have dropped a few games here and there, but it looks like I will make the finals on Saturday. I don't see anyone in my flight who will give me much trouble. And I have won this tournament the last several years."

Cheryl, showing her obvious adulation of Eric, replied, "I didn't realize that, Mr. Shoemaker. This is only my first year here."

"How is your schoolwork going?" he asked, just to keep her talking so he could continue to ogle.

"I'll be a senior this year," Cheryl said.

"That's great. Have you decided on a college yet?"

"I've been looking into Auburn and Tulane. I really want to get out of Houston." Actually, she had not seriously looked anywhere yet, but had heard other members talking about these schools, and she wanted Eric to know she wanted her independence.

"You know, I went to UVA," his pompous attitude lost on her, "but it's very expensive, especially for out-of-state students."

"Maybe I'll check into it, too." Cheryl wanted to show interest but knew nothing about Northern schools. Having grown up in Houston, everything north of the Gulf Coast states was considered the North.

"Well, Richmond was the capital of the South, honey, so be careful what you call *Northern* if you go there," Eric teased.

She laughed coyly, not knowing what he meant by *capital of the South*. She wasn't really good at geography and didn't want to appear dumb.

"Let me know if you're serious about UVA. I might can help."

Craig knew Eric wouldn't give her an ounce of help with UVA and had heard enough of his flirting, so he decided to end it. "Cheryl, did you unpack those T-shirts yet?"

"No, sir, Mr. Fitzgerald. You asked me to fill in with Mrs. Rossin's group and I just finished. I'll get to it now." She turned to Eric, "I'd like to talk to you about UAV. Thanks, Mr. Shoemaker."

Eric held his amusement at her faux pas. "Any time, Cheryl."

"So, Mr. Shoemaker." Craig always called members he didn't care for by their last name. Eric was clueless about the practice. "What do you make of the new kid in the tournament, Daniel Furman?" Craig noticed a little redness creep up Eric's neck.

Eric answered dryly, "He hasn't won a set by better than 6-4 and he's lost a few sets 6-4, so I guess he's hanging in there by a thread. Billy or David will probably knock him out, so I won't have the pleasure of doing it myself. That's too bad."

He left the pro shop and headed for the locker room. The mention of Daniel put him in a bad mood, and he was ready for a shower.

"Hey, Clark," Craig motioned to his assistant pro, "What do you think of Daniel's games?"

Clark was from England, a product of the public tennis system there, and he was becoming an excellent teaching pro. The clients loved his accent, and he loved to flirt with the women. And he ran a very well-organized clinic.

"He's sort of a puzzle. He has great mechanics but doesn't hit the ball particularly hard, and he will put together four or five good shots and then dump one into the net. His serve is good, but he hits it right into the opponent's strong shot. You'd think he'd see that and hit it away."

"I wasn't asking about that, Clark. I meant his game scores," Craig said.

"Oh. Daniel seems to be getting better as he moves through the tournament, since he only won against some of the easier players by 6-4. I think he will have to step up his game to get by Billy or David."

"Really? I bet I can predict the exact scores of both of those matches. Bet a cheeseburger on it?"

"Sure," Clark said. Food was free from the canteen for the pros, so losing the bet just meant he would have to go get it.

"I'll write it down and put it in the drawer."

"How can you be so positive?" Clark asked.

"Look at the pattern of his wins and losses, set by set. He has set up a little rhythm to it, like he's toying with the opponents, and he's bored, so his entertainment is winning and losing when he wants to. The opponents have nothing to do with it."

"But they all seem to enjoy the matches."

"That's the best part. He gives them a great time, some of them even think they have a chance to win, and they are all playing above their normal level, so they are loving it. But he is dictating every game."

"Will he beat Billy and David?" Clark asked.

"That's not an issue. The question is, what will he do with Eric?" Craig said.

"Why Eric?"

"Did you see Eric's reaction when I asked him about Daniel?"

The subtlety of the Southern genteel language was lost on Clark, so he just shrugged.

"Well, there's no love lost there," Craig insisted.

"You've just described half the members' feelings about Eric," Clark laughed.

"Is 'half' another of your British understatements?" Craig laughed along with Clark, and they headed to the canteen for an afternoon snack.

CHAPTER 21

the showdown

"Hey Clark, where's my cheeseburger?" Craig hollered from across the patio of the Westmoreland Country Club tennis arena.

"Oh, yeah, I forgot to look at your sheet. Were you right?" Clark asked.

"Dead on the money. I still can't figure out what he's going to do with Eric, but he played Billy and David to perfection," Craig said.

"I know, I was watching along with everyone else. Not many people watched Eric, though. I'll get your burger and then go get the court ready. We're short one line judge; can I use Cheryl?" Clark asked.

"I'd rather not. We don't need the distraction on the court. See if you can get Helen's son, Spencer. He's got good eyes."

"Good idea. I take it you'll be the chair umpire?"

"Yep. Victor wouldn't let me out of it," Craig lamented. "Tell them to put Old Bay on the fries. I'll be at Center Court. Thanks, Clark."

Craig saw Daniel heading toward the locker room and sidled up beside him. "You've had some long matches, Daniel, especially the last one against Billy. I hope it didn't wear you out for your match with Eric."

"Billy is very consistent and has some great shots. I think he would have given Eric a real run for his money."

"Yeah. Eric seems to have had a pretty easy time of it so far," Craig said.

"Yep. I hope I can give him a good game," Daniel responded coolly.

"Right," Craig said sarcastically and smiled. "I have a feeling it's going to be a bit different than the others."

"Maybe. We'll see soon enough." Daniel's tone gave nothing away.

"The grass is in great shape, so you should have a fast match—pace-wise, that is." Craig searched Daniel's expression for any hints, but Daniel was as stone-faced as ever, acting nonchalant.

"Should be fun on the grass. I'm looking forward to playing on it," Daniel said, as if it was just another Saturday afternoon pick-up game.

"Was that Phillip Rogers I saw in the stands earlier?" Craig was still fishing. He knew Phillip well, but wanted to see if Daniel was aware of him.

"Who?" Daniel said absentmindedly, as if he had barely heard the question.

"Phillip Rogers, the pro out at Galveston. Looked like one of the young Rice players was with him."

"Don't know," Daniel said. "I guess I better start getting ready. Preliminaries in half an hour?"

"Yeah, Daniel. See you out there." Craig grinned as Daniel walked away. *He's got ice in his veins,* Craig thought as Clark came up with his cheeseburger.

The grass was impeccable, as was all of Center Court, the jewel of Westmoreland Country Club. Victor had ordered it closed for a week in preparation for this event, the finale of two weeks of tournament play and other festivities including golf, croquet, bocce, and bridge tournaments. The gala after the tennis finals was attended by almost every member of the club, and their guests were often the who's who of Texas. The alcohol flowed freely, and the women's hats competed for outrageousness.

• • •

Daniel and Eric carefully avoided each other before the match, Daniel quietly attending to his own preparation while Eric was working the members and guests, shaking hands and doling out bravado in an inexhaustible stream. Finally, the time came for the grand entrance onto the court. Victor, as the host and emcee, made the introductions. Daniel was introduced first and walked onto the court, shook hands with Victor, waved to Sarah, set down his two small racquet covers, and then proceeded to the net to await Eric's introduction. Eric, being the defending club champion, was then introduced and came boisterously onto the court with his huge bag, carried like a knapsack and stuffed with six freshly strung racquets wrapped in plastic, plenty of shirts—all from the pro shop and sporting the Westmoreland logo—and his own unique blend of sports drinks, which he arranged by his bench in perfect order. He shook Victor's hand, turned and waved to the crowd, and went to the net for the spinning of the racquet to determine who served first.

As a long-standing tradition, the racquet was an old Spalding used by Pancho Gonzales and sporting his signature. For the toss, the signature side was up and the other side down. Eric made the call, and Craig spun the racquet and let it settle onto the grass. The signature was up and Eric had called down, so Daniel won the right to serve first. He immediately gave the serve to Eric and selected a side, then went to his bench, unzipped his racquet cover, and removed his racquet.

"You better hope you don't break a string," Eric laughed derisively when he saw the one modern racquet Daniel had.

"I'm sure someone will loan me a racquet if I do," Daniel returned.

Eric made a show of removing several of his racquets, looking them over and testing the grips, and then selecting one and removing the plastic wrap. He hit the base of his palm a couple of times, as if ensuring the tension of the strings was perfect, and headed out to his side of the court. Daniel had pretended to tie his shoes while Eric put on his performance, and he stepped onto the court after Eric was at his baseline. Craig opened two cans of balls, positioned the ball boys and girls, and tossed a ball to Eric to begin the warm-ups. Daniel returned five shots matching the exact speed and spin as Eric delivered them, and then hit one long. Craig tossed a ball to Daniel as the ball boy gathered the long ball and rolled it to the ball girl stationed near Craig. Daniel again returned five shots, and then hit the tape.

Craig counted each set of warm-ups, quickly got Daniel's pattern and smiled. Eric's confidence was growing with each of Daniel's perfect misses. After a few net volleys and lobs, with overheads, each of Daniel's copying Eric's, Craig announced service practice and tossed three balls to each ball retriever for delivery to the players. Daniel again emulated each of Eric's serves, but besides Craig, only two other people were aware of it—Phillip and Andersen, who had been given guest tickets by Sarah. Finally, Craig announced that play begin and opened two new cans and had the balls delivered to Eric.

Eric tossed a ball up while holding his racquet behind his back, and hit it flat with all of his effort. Daniel did not move a muscle as the serve went long, the line judge indicating the miss with an outstretched hand. Eric served his second, this one slower with some top spin, and Daniel took one step, returned an easy forehand to Eric, and then stepped to the middle baseline. Eric hit a booming topspin forehand down the line and Daniel effortlessly cross-over stepped to it and returned a topspin cross-court backhand, which Eric ran down and hit back to the middle of Daniel's court. Daniel was already in position and returned it to Eric's forehand, causing him again to turn cross-court for the return. After several more, Eric finally hit one into the tape, and the ball dribbled back onto his side of the court.

"Love, fifteen," Craig announced. After just one point, Eric was breathing heavily and had perspiration on his forehead. Eric went to the ad court and served. This time his first serve was on the money, and he ran in behind it for the half-volley put-away. Daniel hesitated just for a split second, allowing Eric to commit, then turned his racquet slightly and lobbed over him. Eric slid to a halt on the grass and scrambled back to retrieve the lob. His weak return went to Daniel, who was positioned at his service line, waiting. Instead of hitting the easy put-away, he again started his forehand/backhand hits, causing Eric to run back and forth. Finally, Daniel hit one a foot past the baseline. The line judge called out and raised an arm to his side.

"Fifteen-fifteen," Craig announced. And so the game continued, Daniel calmly moving to Eric's shots and running him relentlessly until Eric missed or Daniel decided to give up the point. After two deuce points, Eric pulled out a win and fist pumped as he changed sides, stopping for a sports drink along the way. Sweat was dripping from the end of his nose, and he grabbed a towel, wiped down and threw the towel to the ball girl before proceeding back onto the court.

Daniel was already at the service line, bouncing a ball calmly as he waited for Eric to get into position. Daniel stepped to the service line, positioned the ball on the throat of the racquet, started his downward motion, which smoothly transitioned into a perfect ball toss as his racquet moved continuously in a sweep down his back and came up and over his head to meet the ball as it began its downward flight. He launched the ball with a small amount of topspin to Eric's easy forehand return. Daniel was waiting and hit his backhand to Eric's backhand, and the running by Eric began all over again. The crowd was enjoying the long points, the perfect lobs by Daniel whenever Eric tried to approach the net, or the occasional passing shot winners when Daniel needed the point to pull even and prolong the game. They were dismayed, however, by the score. Daniel could not seem to win a game. Although the first set took a long time to complete, Eric clearly was coming out ahead in every game and won the first set 6-0.

Craig was trying not to smile as he watched Eric's pace slow as his legs became leaden with fatigue. Daniel had not yet picked up a towel and drank only a cup of water at each changeover. Eric had nearly consumed his entire stash of sports drinks. The next set went along similarly to the first and the crowd got restless, seeing that although the tennis was good, Daniel was going to lose in straight sets. At the 5-0 changeover, Eric was on top of the world, fist-pumping and holding up one finger as he went to his bench.

"Eric," Daniel asked as he was sitting down, slowly untying his shoe, "how much is your charity?"

"Ten thousand dollars," Eric said slowly, enunciating each syllable, and ensuring as many people as possible heard. "To the ASPCA."

"Is that all?" Daniel said, feigning surprise.

"What do you mean?" Eric said defensively. "How much is yours?"

"Forty thousand," Daniel said quickly, just loud enough for the first rows to hear.

"What?" Eric was truly surprised. He always bragged about giving the most each year and not only winning the tournament, but also having his name on the charity plaque in the entrance hall. His anger surfaced quickly as he heard Daniel announce his amount. Most tournament participants gave $500 or $1,000 to their charity, and each made out a check and announced it as they were defeated and left the court. Eric's $10,000 had always received a roar from the crowd when he wrote the final check as the tournament winner and announced his charity. Now, Eric realized, Daniel would steal the crowd's accolades when he announced his amount, and by comparison, Eric's charity would seem paltry.

"I guess when I write the final check, it will set a new record for charity, huh?" Daniel smirked.

"The winner writes the final check, butthead," Eric returned, "And with one game to go, that will obviously be me."

"I doubt it," Daniel said, "but just to make things interesting and save you some money, I'll pay your $10,000 if you do win, if you'll pay my $40,000 if I win. After all, it is just charity. Is that legal, Victor?" Daniel said, just to make sure Eric would lose face if he declined.

Victor was sitting in the front box, mid-court, with the governor and a member of Congress. He held up two manila envelopes and said, "Well, you both have contracts for your charity, which I have here to include with the checks. If you want to co-sign the contracts, then it's legal. I'll announce it."

Daniel shrugged as if it was no big deal, which further incensed Eric. "Heck, my first check from TGP will cover the charity anyway."

Fuming, Eric blurted, "Well, why don't you just double it, then?"

"Good idea!" Daniel hopped on the offer. "After all, it's great for the charity, and the crowd will love it." He had just played to all of Eric's narcissistic pressure points, and Eric had responded to each one. Victor smiled, knowing Daniel had taken his advice to study narcissism before Saturday. *The kid does his homework,* Victor thought.

Eric had no choice but to sign or be derided by the entire crowd as news of the exchange was riffling through it. The crowd, which had been lulled into a fatalistic air of the inevitable, was coming to life as the gauntlet was thrown down.

Daniel finished removing his shoes and walked toward Victor to sign the contracts.

"What the hell are you doing?" Eric said, looking at Daniel's bare feet.

Daniel shrugged, waited for Eric to scrawl his name, and chided back, "I don't need shoes to beat you." At that moment he opened his old tennis cover and pulled out an antique Donnay wooden racquet. "And this should do just fine, also."

By now Eric was apoplectic with rage at Daniel's insolence. "Get ready to write a $100,000 check, asshole!"

"I doubt it, Mr. Shoemaker," Daniel said, dripping with politeness, but letting Craig have a piece of enjoyment by using Eric's last name. "By the way, my contract states that every ace is worth $1,000 to the charity. Do you want yours to your forehand or backhand side?"

"You can't ace me with your measly serve, you shithead!"

"Forehand it is, then," Daniel said and headed back onto the court. "And you can forget about abusing baseball players next year. My charity creates Lockwood Youth Baseball Foundation and gives me veto power over all coach selections. And we won't be stacking teams."

This brought a round of applause from the crowd, many of whom had children in the league.

"I'm going to kill him!" Eric said as he stormed back onto the court.

"Hey, Victor," Craig said, "was the Swede's signature on that racquet?"

"Sure as hell was," Victor responded. "A present to Daniel's dad after the Swede won at Wimbledon."

"Son-of-a-bitch," was all Craig could muster.

Daniel handed his glasses to the ball girl and took four balls from her, handling each for a moment until he had the two with the most life remaining, and bounced the others back to the girl. He then turned his hat around to get the brim out of his way and stepped up to the baseline. His service motion was the same smooth stroke as all of his previous serves, except this time he came across the top of the ball and exploded onto it, his feet leaving the ground by nearly a foot.

The Donnay imparted an incredible energy to the ball. Spinning at over two thousand RPMs, the ball curved sharply as it crossed the net, hit in the service court, kicked up at a sharp angle, and cracked against the back wall. Eric had barely been able to move a step toward it before it was past him, well out of reach. The speed clock registered one hundred eighteen miles per hour, its first time into triple digits, and the crowd was suddenly on their feet. Eric shot a glance at Daniel and shouted, "What the f—" but didn't get the profanity out as Craig announced as loud as he could, "Fifteen-love, ace number one."

Eric immediately ran to Victor. "Victor, is this a con or what? He can't serve like that! Nobody can serve like that!"

"Professionals do it every day, Eric, and you're always telling people how you could be on the circuit if you wanted. So, let's see you return one." Victor motioned him back on the court. "And Eric, with a modern racquet, that serve would top one hundred thirty miles an hour."

"I'm not going to stand for this, Victor. It's cheating!"

"Cheating? The kid is barefoot with a wooden tennis racquet and you're up here crying? Craig, tell Daniel to serve whether Eric is in position or not."

"Shit!" was all Eric could say as he ran back onto the court. Daniel motioned to Eric's backhand side, tossed the ball and hit a flat serve three feet up the side of the outside service line and six inches in. The speed clock registered one hundred twenty-three miles per hour, and the crowd went wild. Eric threw his racquet at the net. Daniel gave him time to retrieve it, and when he was close to the net said, "I'll give you one you can hit now. And, Eric, you're not good enough to get mad at your game."

"Fuck you!"

Daniel kept his word and gave Eric a ninety-mile-per-hour serve to his forehand, following the serve in toward the net with a fluidity that made it seem like he was floating. Eric took the forehand and pounded it back at Daniel, who half-volleyed it from inside the service line toward Eric's backhand side, half a court away from his reach.

"By the way, Eric, that's how you come in behind a serve." The crowd cheered the shot as Craig announced forty-love. "This one is into your body, so keep your racquet up!" Daniel sauntered back to the service line, set up, and hit a heavy topspin serve directly at Eric. The kick-serve bounced high and Eric reacted with his racquet over his head, but the speed of the ball turned his out-of-control racquet to jelly, and the ball ricocheted off his frame into the crowd.

"Game," Craig announced, "Score is five games to one. Eric's serve."

By now Eric had retrieved some of his wits and decided all he needed to do was win one of his service games and this nightmare would be over. After all, he had not lost his serve the entire tournament. His first serve was a decent shot out wide. But Daniel was moving into position as the ball was coming off Eric's racquet, so he easily took the forehand return down the line, with pace and massive topspin Eric had never seen before. It bounced near the baseline, then hit the back wall before he could get close to it.

"Love-fifteen," Craig announced. The crowd had now hushed, keying in on Daniel's next shot.

Eric tried a wide-out serve to Daniel's backhand, but Daniel also was anticipating that—he was in perfect position for his one-handed topspin backhand down the other side of the court for a clear winner. He was turning away from Eric toward the deuce court to receive the next serve before the ball had bounced for the second time. Eric had barely made it to the center line. Craig's voice boomed, "Love-thirty." Eric decided he could get Daniel with a hard serve down the middle and come in behind it. The serve bounced off the center line, and as Eric raced in for the half volley, Daniel chipped a backhand drop shot that cleared the net by inches, away from Eric's forehand, and had so much backspin it bounced backward off the grass into the net, making it impossible for Eric to return even if he could have gotten to it. His legs were so heavy with fatigue now that every movement felt like he was pulling a freight train.

"Love-forty."

Eric had one more trick he decided to try. When opponents were standing too far behind the baseline in order to return his big, weekender serve, he would serve an underhand drop-shot as close to the net as he dared, and the opponent would rarely be able to get to it. When they did, they would usually miss the return shot, since they were charging so hard just to get near it. Daniel saw Eric drop his elbow and instantly was on the move to the net. By the time the shot cleared the net, Daniel was a step away from it and easily took it with a short backhand with side spin at a sharp angle to Eric's backhand side, and Eric was left helplessly chasing it, swinging at air as it bounced into the player benches. He threw his racquet at the bench as Craig announced, "Game, two-five."

"This is ridiculous, Victor!" Eric shouted, "This is a con job and you know it! There's no way I'm going to pay this shyster's charity. I'll sue his ass first."

"That's your choice, Eric. You should have done your homework. If you had, you would have discovered that Daniel, also known as 'Trip' Furman, was the top college player last year and lost a three-setter in the finals to Heath Whitman, who is now on the tour ranked in the top twenty-five. Trip is on the cover of one of the older magazines in the pro shop."

"That means he's not eligible for this tournament!" Eric shot back, finding a glimmer of hope.

"Trip Furman is a former college player, just like Billy and David. He never turned pro, and his father was a charter member here, so Daniel was born with a lifetime membership. Also, you should have read the contracts. If you quit, that's breach of contract and cause for immediate dismissal from VCM and forfeiture of all monies vested. Be careful with what you're about to do."

Eric was now totally consumed with fear and humiliation. With the two aces Daniel had handed him, he would owe $102,000 if he lost the match. He was already deeply in debt with his large house, leased luxury cars, and kids in private school. He was planning to use a new credit card to cover the $10,000 charity, and he had been banking on landing the TGP contract to cover his enormous spending, but now that was gone. If he quit, he would lose his job and vested interest in VCM, which at payout time would be $2 million with his present commissions. If he stayed, he would not be able to cover the $102,000, which would be breaching the contract anyway, so he would lose. His house of cards had just crumbled, and it was all Daniel's fault. Eric wondered where the hell this beast had come from and why he was ruining his life. Eric picked up his car keys and headed out.

"I quit!" he said to Craig as a stunned silence fell over Centre Court. Then the booing started.

Daniel sat sullenly as Eric left the court. He had humiliated Eric just as Eric had humiliated his own son and anyone else unlucky enough to be in his sphere of control. But the feeling that overcame Daniel was quite different than the sweetness of revenge he had anticipated.

CHAPTER 22

bitter revenge

"Daniel? Daniel, are you in there?"

Daniel heard Sarah's call and looked around the Westmoreland Country Club locker room. It was empty, and from his vantage point sitting on the floor, he could tell the stalls were also empty.

"Yes, Sarah. Come on in. It's clear," Daniel said.

Sarah cautiously stepped into the doorway. "You sure it's okay?"

"Yes," Daniel said, quiet resignation apparent in his reply.

"I've never been in a men's locker room before." She did not want the tone of Daniel's voice to dampen her elation, so she barged in. "That was a great performance out there! What a rock star! You had the crowd mesmerized, and you so put Eric in his place! They've never seen tennis like that at this club, even on the grass. Now they know what real tennis looks like."

"No, they don't. That was bullshit." Daniel cut her off.

"What do you mean? What is wrong with you? You handed him his head on a platter and totally humiliated him. Quite deservedly, too!"

"Exactly, Sarah. And who the hell do I think I am to do that to him?"

"After all the crap that narcissistic bastard has dished out? You're feeling sorry for him?"

"No, that's not it at all."

"Well, then *what's* the problem? The party's going on, and you haven't even showered and changed yet! They're all waiting for you out there."

"They'll have to wait. I'm going to slip out the back and head to Galveston."

"Daniel! You can't do that! What is wrong with you? I don't understand you at all. For the past month you've been setting up this showdown, and now you're just going to slink away? Even Victor is hanging around for the party. You can't just leave!"

Sarah put her back to the cold tile wall and slid down to sit on the floor beside Daniel. "Talk to me, Daniel. What's the real issue?"

"My question is serious. Who am I to act like that just to humiliate another human being? I'm not his daddy. I don't have any right to punish him like that."

"Are you forgetting how he treated Jonathan, or Jennifer, or his own son? He got what he deserved, and in spades!"

"That's just the point. Everyone out there is celebrating revenge. Half the crowd has been at the brunt of Eric's behavior at one time or another, and I'm sure they loved seeing him get his ass kicked. And they are thinking, like you, I should be celebrating a great victory. But I'm truly ashamed of what I did. Yeah, the sweet smell of revenge is in the air, but I'm afraid the Bible is right—revenge belongs to God, not me. I'm no better than Eric now. Revenge is easy and feels good and men relish it, but now I know it's putrid. I'm just not smart enough to know what else to do. What if—?" Daniel paused, as if a mental block had dropped over him.

"What if what?" Sarah prodded.

Daniel finally broke his silence. "You know, I've been so angry with Eric since I first saw him on the baseball field, blasting Benjamin. I think it reminded me of the anger I had at Mom's boyfriend who took the fun out of baseball for me. And that anger has been building ever since. I focused on tennis with Dad, and that just delayed the feelings.

I think Dad knew something about that, and he was trying to warn me the last time I saw him. But I was too selfish—no, too self-centered and stupid—to stop, sit, and listen. All I wanted to do was get away from him. And now here I am, sitting in a locker room feeling like shit. And deservedly so, to use your words."

"I didn't realize you were so angry. You mask it well. No one had any idea," Sarah said.

"Yeah, that might be a trait I got from Dad that isn't as virtuous as it should be. But the poker face has its value on the court. Look, I don't want to bore you with this. It's my problem and my issue. You need to go out there and enjoy the party."

"Don't insult me," Sarah said. "I'm going to sit here and listen until *we* figure this out. I know I talk a lot, but I can listen, too. And I respect our friendship far too much to just walk out and have fun. Now, talk to me. They're all pretty drunk by now anyway, so they won't miss us. I may be the only one who missed you anyway." Sarah looked at her wine glass and noticed she hadn't touched it since she came in. The slight buzz she had was wearing off and the floor was getting very hard and cold, but she didn't want to move. She felt the catharsis in this young man's life and was glad she was there. Now, if she could only be silent.

Daniel sat quietly for a while, trying to organize his thoughts. There were so many paths this conversation could take, and he wanted to go down all of them at once, afraid he would miss one if he didn't. He was paralyzed by indecision and knew he had to just jump in and start swimming. Finally, he went back to his beginnings and the pent-up words started flooding out.

"You know, I hated Mom's boyfriend, but it really wasn't his fault. There was no way he could ever live up to my dad, and he really tried, but everything he did was wrong. He just didn't know any better. He thought tough love was what I needed, but it didn't matter. I was going to hate whatever he did because I loved my father so much. I quit baseball to punish him, which worked out anyway because then I could focus on tennis, which he hated and Dad loved. So, Dad coached me through college. He made me redshirt for a year and graduate early so I would be eligible to play while I was working on my master's degree. I think he was hoping I would mature a little, too."

"So why Stanford?" Sarah immediately regretted asking the question and willed herself into silence, but Daniel didn't miss a beat or seem to mind. His answer flowed as if it was what he was going to say next anyway.

"I think that was me running away. I've always wanted to run. It's as if I think I'm going to find something somewhere else. I ran from baseball and found tennis and my dad, but then I ran from Florida to California because it was so far from my mom. Fortunately, Dad was in San Francisco a lot, so he kept close tabs on my game and my progress. He also was very good friends with my coach there, so he could orchestrate my career. Unfortunately, I found no solace there, and I think my anger just festered. You know, I had a major meltdown in the finals and lost the match."

"I heard, but nobody seems to know about it here," Sarah said.

"I changed as much as I could to hide it. Cut my hair, shaved the beard, started wearing glasses I don't even need. Dropped my nickname and started going by Daniel. Sometimes I still forget to answer when someone calls me. I'm really thankful Dad wasn't around to see it, but I wonder sometimes if I would have gone ballistic if he had been there. He was like the anchor in my life, along with Mishael. I really miss her. Not a day goes by I don't think of her."

Daniel felt the path of his thoughts forking and fought not to get sidetracked. He wanted Sarah to know everything he was feeling, but felt impotent to say it all. He looked at her and felt her patient demeanor. *Must be her age,* he thought. *I would have quit listening a long time ago.*

He waited for her to prod him on, but she remained quiet. "Anyway, I ran from California to Houston, still not knowing why or what to look for. Just ran for the sake of running, maybe. Or because I didn't know what else to do. It seemed like there was always something missing, and one more win was always the answer. But one more win was never enough. I think Dad was trying to find those words for me. Maybe he did plant them, and I just didn't know it at the time. I'll never know. But here is what I do know, Sarah: the only time I've felt joy in my life, besides when I was with Mishael, was when I was with Jonathan in the batting cage and Andersen on the tennis court. And you know, I just realized those are the only times in my life I have been giving. I think my whole life has been training to be number one, which means you have to make everyone else number two. But with Jonathan and Andersen, I really poured out to them without thinking of what I was going to get out of it. It was pure joy, and at the time, I couldn't even define it. I had no words for how I felt. I think that's why this thing with Eric today was so bad. I felt the extreme opposite of joy. That's got to be why revenge is so putrid. People have been seeking revenge for ten thousand years, and nobody is satisfied yet. And today I am as guilty as the worst of them."

"Aren't you being a bit hard on yourself now?" Sarah admonished.

"Maybe. Maybe not. I just know I want to never do anything like this again. And I also know I can't blame anyone else for my anger, my actions, my sins. I am as guilty as any man who is considered evil. We have no hope of peace as long as men act as I did today. I took the easy path of revenge, not the impossible path of—" Daniel paused, searching, "I don't even know what it is. We've lost the peace and have no name for regaining it, no word for it."

"At church they say it's Jesus, but I go for Jonathan's sake and don't even carry a Bible. Maybe I need to listen more there, too. You remember how you taught Jonathan to watch the ball, to know how it was spinning and feel how it was going to move?"

"Yeah, look for the seams," Daniel said.

"I think that's what you've lost, Daniel. You've lost sight of the ball because you aren't looking for the seams."

"Dad said once it was pointless to look for the seams if you're not in the batter's box. I had no idea what he was saying, but now it makes perfect sense."

"Yeah, Daniel, you need to step into the batter's box and look for the seams. Do you know where the batter's box is?"

"I think it's the batting cage with Jonathan and the tennis court with Andersen. I don't think I need to win another tennis match. I need to give back. I need to see the joy, to feel the joy, to know the joy."

"What are you going to do?"

"I think I'm going to go to Galveston and see if Phillip Rogers will let me open a sports clinic there."

"What about VCM?"

"I guess I'll turn in my resignation."

"Victor said you were a short-timer. I was hoping he was wrong. But he's never wrong about people. He also said if Eric doesn't pay up for losing today, he can get rid of him without losing $2 million. I wonder if he put you in that studio hoping you would be his ticket to Eric's demise. But somehow, he knew you wouldn't be there for very long."

"Interesting. And what happens to the ball field if Eric doesn't pay up? I'll probably have to sell the condo to meet that obligation," Daniel said.

"That's already taken care of. Victor put up the money right after he reviewed the contract."

"He saw my contract?" Daniel turned to her, surprised.

"Do you really think Jennifer made all those revisions? Victor had the legal department go through it with a fine-tooth comb. Eric is screwed if he even thinks about not paying his bill. And Victor hopes he won't. Either way, Westmoreland gets a great new baseball field."

"Shit. I had no idea."

"I think Victor knew you weren't going to be here long because he recognized that you don't thrive on the killer instinct. You're way above that."

"Did Victor say that?"

"No, I figured that out on my own. That's one trait you got from your dad you can be proud of, and why Victor and your dad were different, although they were so alike. Your father did not worship the kill, he looked for the seams in the people he was around. And he hit a lot of home runs. We'll miss you at VCM, but maybe I'll bring Jonathan to your clinics. And maybe a cooler of beer to pass the time."

"I'd like that," Daniel said quietly.

They looked at each other as they pushed themselves up off the floor and headed for the door. They could hear the party in full swing in the courtyard. Daniel felt his inner demons fade as he moved close to Sarah, her presence quenching his anger and restlessness. Mishael's music began to swirl through his mind as Sarah found his hand, clutched it, and laid her head against his bicep. Together, they walked out of the locker room, turned away from the party, and headed toward the back gate. The beach at Galveston was waiting for them.

· · ·

Jeffrey, Daniel's studio mate who, at Victor's directive, had been watching Daniel, left the tennis match before the festivities began and went to the parking lot to check his computer. The tracking device he placed on Daniel's Porsche seemed to be getting some interference and Jeffrey had to figure out the problem. He noticed a brown sedan parked near the entrance with its engine running. Jeffrey decided not to go to his car, but instead casually walked around the maintenance building to get closer to the sedan without being noticed. He saw a Middle Eastern man in the driver's seat, looking at his laptop.

Jeffrey went back into the arena area and left by another gate to the parking lot. He went directly to his car, got in quickly, and drove away, turning into the adjacent lot and finding a park near the woods separating this property from the arena parking lot. From his trunk he took out a detector, a small explosive device, and a tracking device. He deftly hopped the fence and slipped through the wooded area back into the arena parking lot. He stayed low between the cars as he made his way to Daniel's Porsche. His scanner detected two tracking devices—his and one other. He squeezed under the low car and found the second device. This is what had been causing the interference. Jeffrey placed the small explosive next to the device to block interference with his, then headed toward the sedan, still staying low.

Jeffrey moved under the adjacent row of cars to the rear of the sedan, and was about to roll under it when he heard Sarah and Daniel coming out of the locker area toward the Porsche. Jeffrey was quiet and motionless as he heard the throaty roar of Daniel's engine come to life.

Daniel chirped a tire as he turned left out of the parking lot. Jeffrey heard the sedan shift into gear and he quickly rolled toward the sedan and put a tracking device with a built-in explosive on the car, and continued to roll to the next car and out of sight before he could be detected by the Middle Eastern man.

Jeffrey watched from under the car as the Middle Eastern man turned left, following Daniel. He ran back through the woods, hopped back over the fence, and got in his car.

Jeffrey opened his laptop and waited a moment before leaving the parking lot. Two blips appeared on his displayed map. He watched as Daniel headed toward Galveston with the tail several blocks behind. Jeffrey's tracking device was working fine now and, at any time, he could destroy the other tracking device and the brown sedan with a command from his cell phone. For now, he just wanted to monitor it. He would follow both cars at a safe distance.

It was time to give Victor a full report.

the end

author's note

Daniel, Sarah, and Victor return in *The Maine Consecration*, the second book in the series. When Daniel learns the fate of his beloved Mishael, he tumbles into a world of terrorism that redirects his relatively tranquil life, placing him at the center of a centuries-old religious conflict where God becomes synonymous with earthly power and wealth, and revenge the only strategy.

In *The Bank,* the third book in the series, Daniel comes to accept his new course in life and becomes embroiled in a world of technology poised to change the course of history and redefine the center of world power. Daniel must choose between challenging the most powerful institution in history and losing everything he has worked so hard to build.

acknowledgments

Thank you to my typist, editor, friend, tennis partner, punctuation guru, first reader, and sympathetic critic, Helen Anspach.

Thank you to my daughter and ardent critic, who helped me smooth out many roughly written passages, Catherine Conner.

Thank you to my pre-readers: Katherine Ringley, Mike Curtis, Jerry Healy, author of *Originally From Dorchester*, and Rick Burkhart, author of *The Stone in My Shoe*.

Thank you to my writing coach, Amanda Rooker of SplitSeed, who never stopped pushing.

A special thank you to my sisters, Laura Scott Rash and Susan Allred, for their help and advice.

Thank you to the helpful and supportive staff at Koehler Publishing for their hard work. Writing is fun but lonely as it is often done in that private garret in the attic, but it takes a team to bring a book to readers, and Koehler's team is first rate.

Thank you to John Koehler for giving me the opportunity to share Looking for the Seams with the world.

CPSIA information can be obtained
at www.ICGtesting.com
Printed in the USA
BVHW071706150421
605031BV00007B/530